Tangled Vines

Tangled Vines

LaVerne Shaw

Library of Congress Control Number:		2011916426
ISBN:	Hardcover	978-1-4653-6494-4
	Softcover	978-1-4653-6493-7
	Ebook	978-1-4653-6495-1

To order additional copies of this book, contact:
Xlibris Corporation
1-888-795-4274
www.Xlibris.com
Orders@Xlibris.com
100740

CHAPTER 1

"Say you're from Ohio, Ma'am?" Jeb Duggins shot a brown stream of tobacco juice over the edge of the wagon seat. Boxes, crates and a trunk rattled in the bed as they rolled along the rutted road.

"Yes. Ohio." Mylena Harris tucked a tuft of sable brown hair back beneath her gray bonnet as the wind began to whip the dust beneath the wagon wheels.

"Think you'll be goin' back there?"

"I don't know—not for a while anyway as I have no money left to go back. I need this job in order to make ends meet right now."

"Yep. I heard about yore husband bein' killed by them Indians when they blockaded the train. Killed David Wilson too—and a young couple that was running away to git married. Too bad."

Mylena felt her blue eyes fill with tears. Her loss was still too new to talk about. Will Harris was not the love of her life—but he was her husband—had been for three years. They had worked her father's Ohio farm until her father died earlier this year. Then Will had gotten the fever to move to Colorado. Flyers advertising land in eastern Colorado for sale had been everywhere in their area. Will, excited at the prospect of a move to a new country, kept on until Mylena had finally given in and agreed to selling her father's farm in Ohio and investing in Colorado land.

Packed at last, they had traveled by train for several days until tragedy struck. An Indian uprising just over the border into Colorado had stopped the train while a terrible battle took place. Will was felled by an Indian arrow. Three other passengers had died as well. Mylena never knew how many train employees were slain. The Indians were apparently seeking food for their starving tribe. They ransacked the boxcars carrying edibles and rode away amid shouts of success. They had left behind a bleeding, torn group of frightened passengers and crew. The engineer was injured but he had managed to start the train and continue on into Callahan before he collapsed.

Mylena and the other older widow, Louise Wilson, had been forced to stay in the local hotel for days until they could hold some kind of Christian funeral for their husbands and bury them in the Callahan cemetery. A large chunk of her money had been spent to do so. Now she really didn't want to even talk about the days just behind her as she shuddered in remembrance. She was no longer interested in Colorado land. With no home, no family, she was lost.

"Looks like rain." Jeb continued chewing as he talked. "But we'll be there pretty quick now. You'll like Roarc Rhynhart. He's a good man—a good rancher and a good farmer. Yes sir!"

Mylena swallowed the lump in her throat. She HAD to like him. She had no other alternative. Her money was almost gone what with the expenses of burying Will in a strange cemetery and staying in the town's only hotel for two weeks.

"I hope you're right." She swiped the tear rolling down her cheek as she gazed into the seemingly barren distance of almost flat land edged with blue mountains in the far distant west.

"There's his place." Jeb pointed his whip as Mylena turned her eyes to survey the scene. A homestead loomed in the distance nestled in tall cottonwood trees. She could make out a barn and other outbuildings as well as a windmill whirling now in the freshening breeze.

"His wife died a couple of years ago. She was a frail little thing and she left him with a young boy of about five or six. I'm sure he'll welcome some female help again."

Nervous now, Mylena could only stare at the residence she would be expected to take care of—if Mr. Rhynhart approved of her.

Jeb pulled the wagon to a standstill in the front yard. Mylena could see a tall man accompanied by a small boy coming to meet them. Dark clouds loomed in the south heralding a rain storm. Wind whipped her skirt as she stepped down from the buggy unaided.

"Hey, Roarc, here's yore helper come to take over fer ye." Jeb slowly climbed from the wagon and began to unload Mylena's things.

Roarc Rhynhart stopped in his tracks as he stared at Mylena.

"What? This isn't the woman I'm expecting! I asked for the older woman."

"Sorry, Roarc, this is the one ya got. Doc Sims clobbered on to the older Miz Wilson.

Said she had been a doctor's daughter and outta know a bit about nursing the sick. This young woman was what was left."

Roarc frowned in irritation. This would never do! Young women did not fare well in this outback of lonely land. Hadn't his dead wife told him that over and over?

"No! Take her back to town!" Roarc roared as he turned away. The little boy grabbed his father's leg and begged.

"No, Papa! You said she would cook us something good for supper! Don't let her go away!"

Horrified at this turn of events, Mylena turned to again mount the wagon but Jeb stopped her with a hand in the air. He shook his head at Roarc Rhynhart.

"I already got her trunk unloaded. It's fixin' t'rain and I'm aheadin' home. See ya!"

Mylena stood transfixed in the dirt path leading to the front porch of the ship-lap house.

Roarc stood with clenched fists as he watched Jeb roll away in the delivery wagon. The man's black hat was pulled low on his brow and she could not see his facial features very well.

Suddenly he turned with a deep frown.

"Well, looks like you're here for the night anyway. Might as well come on in."

He hoisted her trunk atop his broad shoulders as if it weighed nothing and proceeded to lead the way to the front porch. The little boy ran ahead and held the door open for them to enter.

Once inside, Mylena looked about the large room. It was neat with no homey touches.

"You'll sleep in the bedroom. Rian and I will sleep in the loft." He lowered her trunk in the designated bedroom and scowled.

Mylena looked at the room with its iron bedstead and hand sewn quilt. A tall dresser stood on one side of the room with a wavy mirror atop it. A claw-footed table was set beside the bed with a double globed lamp standing ready to be lit in the ensuing gloom. She had never felt so unwelcome in her entire life!

Roarc turned to her and spoke in a gruff voice. "We need supper cooked. I'll show you the kitchen area." He made good his words as he led her back through the large front room to the end where a table and chairs waited beside a cabinet. She noticed a water pump and a sink. That was certainly a plus. He indicated the huge iron stove, the kindling box of wood to fill it's belly and the storage room for supplies. He opened the back door and pointed out the cooling trough where crocks of milk sat in the trickling cold water.

"Come on, Rian, we need to finish our chores. We'll be back in about an hour." Then they disappeared down the back path toward the barn and other outbuildings. Sprinkles of rain began to spatter against the window panes as Mylena turned back to survey this strange scene she found herself enmeshed in.

She made her way back to the bedroom where she took off her cloak then hung her hat on a nail in the wall. She shook out her gray skirt and rolled up the sleeves of her white blouse. She could certainly cook them a meal.

Adept in the kitchen, she soon had a roaring fire going as well as a kettle of water on to heat She began searching for something to cook. In the store room she found a ham hanging. She took it back to the cabinet where she managed to find a sharp knife to slice slabs of the meat. She found potatoes and onions in the storeroom as well. Soon she had a skillet of ham, diced onions and potatoes simmering atop the black stove.

She discovered a granite mixing bowl beneath the cabinet. Flour and baking powder seemed to be on hand as well. Soon she was mixing biscuit dough, rolling and shaping tiny mounds on a metal sheet ready for the oven.

She turned to set the table with plates and silverware. Only tin plates and cups seemed to be in the cupboard. Scoping out the room, she spied a hutch near the front door bearing a set of flowered china. A lower drawer revealed knives, forks and spoons in silver plate. They must have belonged to the dead wife. But they looked like they had not been used in years.

By now the water was hot enough to wash the pieces. Soon she had the table set for three and welcoming aromas permeating the house. No clock seemed to be available but she must have timed the work well for she could hear Rian chattering as the two of them stepped onto the back porch and began to wash up in the granite pan waiting there.

Quickly she placed food on the table and poured tin mugs of milk. Then, swathed in a dish towel acting as an apron, she waited to greet the pair with trepidation.

"Oh, look, Papa! It looks pretty and it smells good!" Rian pulled out a chair and sat down with a hungry look on his small face.

Mylena took the chair across from him with a smile at his enthusiasm. Roarc stood for long minutes surveying the scene. Then, with a frown, he asked, "Are you eating with us?"

"Of course. Where else would I eat?" Mylena had had about enough of his rudeness.

Surprised at her saucy comeback, he too sat down, then bowed his head in a prayer of thanksgiving for their food. At least Mylena was impressed with that.

It was a rather silent meal. Only Rian seemed talkative as Roarc chewed with determination.

At last Mylena rose to add a jar of peach preserves to their meal.

"Where did this come from? Did you bring it?" Roarc frowned as he asked at last.

"No. I found it 'way back on a shelf in the storage room. I wondered if it would still be good. I tasted it and and it is—so enjoy."

"Must be something left over . . . . something we missed." Roarc murmured as he filled a biscuit with the preserves. "Look here, Rian, try this." He handed the biscuit to his son who enjoyed the sweet with a small boy grin.

At last the meal was over and Mylena rose to clean-up. Roarc urged Rian to the rocking chair seated before the small fire in the huge fireplace in the center of the room. But Rian darted beneath his father's arm and ran back to place his small arms about Mylena's waist.

"Thank you for the supper. Papa said you would be a good cook." He smiled up at her and Mylena's heart melted. She hugged the little boy back and felt the bird-like bones of his shoulders and back. He needed fattening up.

But Roarc only stood there, hands in pockets and watched the tableau.

Mylena hung her damp dish towel across the back of a chair to dry. She whipped off her make-shift apron, then made her way to the bedroom where she closed the door with a decided click.

Roarc sat in the rocking chair with Rian in his lap reading from the Bible. This was a plus for the man but his rudeness was certainly not.

She rummaged in her trunk for a night gown, then made use of the small facilities in her bedroom, threw back the hand made quilt and sank into the feather bed. Exhausted from the day's travails, she fell asleep almost immediately. Even the soft patter of the rain drops spattering her one window did not disturb her.

Roarc urged Rian up the loft ladder at last. He banked the fire, checked the black wood stove, then followed his son up the steps to the loft. Rian was cuddled into the feather bed cushioned by fresh hay from the barn.

"Asleep, son?" Roarc whispered. But no answer came so he knew the boy had slipped into a peaceful slumber after a very busy day. Roarc rubbed his jaw, then slipped into bed beside his son. But sleep would not claim him. In his mind's eye he kept seeing the face of the young woman now sleeping in his bed downstairs. Should he ask her to stay on? He really needed someone—but—she was so young. She would not last in this far-flung country. Memories of Lavina assaulted him.

Lavina had been a bride at twenty-five—a bit old for a first marriage. But at the time, she had seemed eager to take on a husband and a home. He had thought he loved her—but had he really? Perhaps he had simply wanted a settled life with a wife and children. Three months into the marriage he had realized he had chosen the wrong woman.

At first she had seemed eager to make the move to Colorado. Sentiment was still running high in Missouri just after the Civil War. Neighbors warred with each other until it was a dangerous place to live. But once they had chosen their land and settled, she was not happy. She complained about their isolation, about the lack of time to socialize with people. She had been a town girl so the hardships of farm/ranch life had been too much for her. Pregnancy had been a bitter pill for her. She had felt doomed to a life of drabness and drudgery. Roarc had felt guilty at the joy he experienced in looking forward to a child of his own.

Strangely enough, Lavina had made it through the birth of their son with flying colors.

Roarc had been so fearful for her but she had seemed relieved of the burden of carrying the child—so relieved that she was a rather cold mother to the baby. Roarc had bonded with the boy immediately.

As the child grew, he became a miniature of Roarc in looks, in actions. Lavina chided them about this declaring she had nothing to do with his heredity at all except for the color of his tawny hair.

Then, when Rian was four, an exceptionally cold winter had arrived. It wiped out most of Roarc's stock. Lavina came down with a bad cold that quickly became pneumonia and culminated in her death. Roarc had felt guilty. If he had been in a town perhaps she might have gotten the necessary medical care and lived. She had so despised their isolation. Perhaps depression had added to her demise. He would never know—but he would probably always feel guilty. He vowed to harness no other young woman to such a life. He and Rian would make it alone!

After all he had four ranch hands living in the bunkhouse and Mose to take care of them. Mose had been a friend of Roarc's father. He was in his fifties with grizzled hair and a bushy gray mustache. He presided over the bunkhouse and its inhabitants. He cooked and did laundry and any other chores necessary to keep the ranch running. But Roarc could tell Mose was growing older and really needed some help. An older live-in woman was what Roarc needed to keep the ranch running smoothly. Besides it was time for Rian to learn to read and cipher. Perhaps a woman could teach him during the long winter months. It was still a sound idea—but the woman who came was much too young! She would never do!

Roarc tossed and turned until the wee hours trying to come to some conclusion.

What should he do? Should he take a chance on the woman—or send her back to town as quickly as he could?

CHAPTER 2

Mylena awoke with the touch of a small hand on her forehead. Instantly her blue eyes took in the small boy standing beside her bed. Mylena sat up in alarm. What time was it? Had she overslept? How awful! That dreadful man—Roarc—didn't want her anyway. Now she really would be in trouble.

"Can you wake up?" the boy asked in a small voice. "Papa said you'd fix me some breakfast."

"Of course I will. Just let me get dressed and I'll be right there."

The boy left the room closing the bedroom door softly behind him. Mylena threw off the covers and scrambled to wash and dress. She shook out the gray traveling skirt and white blouse—not so white now—but they would have to do. She didn't have time to unpack something else to wear. Besides, Roarc Rhynhart would probably be taking her back to town today. She smoothed her hair as best she could and opened the bedroom door. What would she find on the other side?

Rian stood at the front window watching rain run in rivulets down each pane. He turned at her entrance and smiled. Mylena felt her heart melt once more at his angelic smile.

She found the black stove glowing with heat and a pot of coffee waiting. Roarc must have been up early. She probably should have been up much earlier to prepare a meal for him as well.

"What do you want me to fix for your breakfast?" Her smile welcomed his confession.

"I would like pan cakes and syrup. Can you make that?"

"Well I guess. Do you know where the syrup is?" He darted toward the storage room and emerged with a large bottle of dark molasses.

"I found it!" He proudly displayed his prize for her approval.

"Well done! Now let's mix up some batter." Soon Mylena was ladling batter onto the hot metal sheet. Rian stood well back from touching the hot stove but he watched with round eyes as the batter bubbled and Mylena flipped each pancake over with a deft movement. Soon a stack of golden cakes awaited his enjoyment.

Much later, with a smear of syrup on his chin, Rian shared another of his smiles.

"That was really good Miss . . . . what should I call you?"

"Well, how about Miss Mylena? Can you manage that all right?"

"But I thought you was a married lady."

"Well—I was. But my husband was killed by Indians so I'm what is called a widow now. That's a lady with no husband any more."

"I know about that. My Papa don't have any wife any more but I forget what they call him. You know since he hasn't got a wife and you got no husband maybe you could be our family."

Mylena gave a quick shake of her sable head.

"Probably not, Rian. People have to be married to be a family."

"Oh-h-h . . ."

Both heads turned as they heard Roarc clearing his throat at the back door. He was taking off his boots and entering the room. Had he heard their conversation? Mylena felt her face flushing at the thought that he might have been listening.

Into the small pool of silence, he declared, "It's raining cats and dogs out there. We can't make a trip to town today. It will be solid mud all the way."

"Would you like some coffee?" Mylena tried to cover her embarrassment with this suggestion.

"Sure . . . and did I hear Rian say pancakes? I'd like to try some of them too."

While Roarc ate, Rian regaled him with Mylena's cooking skills. She found a bag of pinto beans in the store room and settled down to prepare them for cooking. Rainy days called for a big pot of beans to her way of thinking. Since they weren't going back to town today, she would be able to finish them and maybe stir up a pan of cornbread too.

Mylena had little to say to the autocratic man seated at the table drinking a final cup of coffee. At last he rose, touched his mouth with a handkerchief and nodded to Mylena as she stood at the sink.

"Very good, Mrs. Harris. Thank you."

But she could only nod and give a brisk acknowledgment of his words. He might be the best looking male she had ever seen but he was far too rude to her way of thinking. His manners were atrocious. Soon he was swinging out the door.

"Better stay in a little longer, Rian, it's still raining some out here."

Once she had cleared the table again, Mylena wished for some apples.

"Why do you want apples?" Rian was always inquisitive.

"Oh if I had some apples I could make a pie."

"Well—I know where there are some!" He scampered away and disappeared into the dark recesses of the storage room. Soon he emerged with an apple in each hand.

"You really found some! But I would need more than two . . . . " He scampered away again to return with two more apples.

"If you can find two more we can have that pie, young man." Mylena's laughter echoed around the cozy room. Rian again disappeared and returned with two more shiny red apples.

"Where did you get these?" she wanted to know.

"Papa keeps them hidden in straw so we can have some now and then."

"Will he mind if we use these?"

"Oh no! If you're making a pie he sure 'nuff won't. Can I help?"

Rian was fascinated with the peeling of the apples. Mylena could peel an apple without breaking the curl of the peel. "We'll save those for the chickens," she declared as the peels were piled in a generous heap atop the cabinet. Next she mixed dough and rolled it out in circles. Rian watched avidly as she punched one layer into the metal pan, then added the sliced fruit and topped it with the other layer of dough. She sprinkled sugar on top and gently slid the concoction into the wood stove's interior.

"Now we must watch to see the stove is kept burning at the same heat so the pie will bake evenly." Rian stood beside the wood box impatiently but it was a long while before Mylena finally declared the pie done and slipped it from the oven. It smelled delicious. Rian was ready to taste it right now but Mylena insisted the pie was far too hot to eat yet. With a groan the little boy turned away and stared out the window once more.

"It's still raining. I'm tired of rain. I wanta see about the chickens and gather some eggs. Besides I need to go see Olga in the barn."

"And who is Olga?" Mylena wondered if there was another female on the place after all. She had noticed several figures running through the rain but had not met any of them.

"Olga's our dog. She's gonna have pups any day now and I don't wanta miss seeing them. She lives in the barn 'cause Papa doesn't like animals in the house much."

"Maybe tomorrow the sun will shine and you can do all those things." Mylena tried to dispel his dejection.

"I just wish I could write my name. Them Grady boys can all write their names and they laugh at me 'cause I can't."

"Who are the Grady boys?"

"Their Pa works for my Papa and they live in a house down by the wheat field. There's three of them—Joe, Sam, and Jim. They've been to school."

"No wonder they can write their names. They are all only three letters."

"Could you teach me to write my name?" Rian's eyes were huge in his small face.

"I'll bet I could. What is your real name and how is it spelled?"

"I don't know but it's all written down here in Papa's Bible." He immediately lifted the black book from Roarc's desk in the corner. Gingerly Mylena took the book and found the center pages that bore testimony of the family's births, marriages and deaths written in a spidery hand.

She ran a finger down the page until she found what she was looking for: Rian Alexander Rhynhart born August 17th. She also spied the inscription: Roarc Charles Rhynhart born May 20th . . . . then there were other, older family members listed. In the opposite column deaths were noted. The last one was Lavina Curtis Rhynhart with the date written just two short years ago.

Curiosity got the best of Mylena. "Was Lavina your mother?"

"Ummhmm. But I don't ever 'member her. I was too little when she died."

How sad Mylena reflected. He must have been about three. "Don't you remember anything at all about her?"

"Sometimes I remember sitting on her lap while she combed my hair . . . . and sometimes she sang to me but that's all . . . . " He wandered back to his dad's desk and came back with a piece of paper and a stubby pencil.

"Is my name hard to write?"

"No it isn't. Sit here beside me and I'll show you." Rian scooted in the rocking chair beside Mylena as she took the pencil and paper.

"First there is an R"—she drew one line. "Here is his first leg. Then he has a fat stomach"—and she drew a pouch. "And last is his other leg—see?" Rian nodded in awe.

"An R makes a growling sound." Mylena proceeded to match her vocal sounds to her words. Rian giggled.

"Next is just a long, tall man standing still." She drew an I as Rian watched. "He doesn't say anything yet. But next to him is a lady." She drew an A. "She has two legs and an apron that will hold apples for a pie." Rian laughed out loud. "What does she say?"

"She says 'Aahh'."

"Is that all the letters?"

"Oh no. The last letter is the gate to their farm. It looks like this." She drew two lines and joined them with a cross bar. "When the cross bar is down no one can come in without their permission. That is called an N and it says nnnnnnnnn."

"What is 'permission'?" Rian's eyes were saucers in his small face.

"That means it's all right for them to come in."

"Oh."

"Now that says RIAN. Let me show you how to make them yourself." She handed him the pencil and guided his small hand as he copied her letters exactly. After several tries, she sat him at the table with instructions to write the letters over and over while she mixed up a pan of cornbread. Later when he showed her the paper, she discovered he had written the cross bar of the N wrong several times

"Oh here's a problem. If the cross bar is on the wrong side, an animal or a mean person could step over it and come right in. You don't want that!" She showed him again the correct way to connect the N. He sat down once more and worked until he had it right.

An early dusk was falling when Roarc stomped onto the back porch, shucked off his muddy boots and came inside in sock feet. Rian immediately ran to take him his "house shoes" made of soft leather and well-worn.

"Thanks, son. Something sure smells good."

"Miss Mylena made us an apple pie! Hurry and wash, Papa, and let's try it."

In the loft later Roarc blew out the lamp and settled down to sleep. It had been a long and arduous day working calves in the rain but they had completed the job. Tomorrow he hoped for sunshine. He stretched his tired legs into a comfortable position and closed his eyes to sleep.

But before he could nod off, a small hand touched his shoulder.

"Papa, I like Miss Mylena. Can she stay?"

"Umm, we'll talk about it later, son."

Rian sat up and shook his father's shoulder. "No, Papa, tomorrow you'll forget. I want her to stay. She cooks good things—and she laughs a lot—and she smells like flowers—and—well I just like her. Can she, Papa? Stay I mean?"

Roarc groaned. Did they have to settle this issue right now? Apparently Rian would not be satisfied without some definite answer.

"Okay, son, I'll talk to her tomorrow. Now, can we go to sleep?"

"Do you promise, Papa?" Rian was still not placated.

"Yes, I promise. Now go to sleep!"

Mylena was awakened by a rooster crowing loudly outside her window. She roused in the dim light of early morning with a smile. If the rooster was up and about, the sun should be shining soon. She threw off her covers and slid to the floor. Soon she was diving into her trunk for something to wear. She pulled out a green print dress—not old, not new—and donned it hastily. She pulled back her sable hair and tied it with a green ribbon. Not too neat but it would do for today. As she left the room she wondered if she would be going or staying here today. If the autocratic Roarc had his way—and he probably would—she would be going. Was she glad? Well—she still desperately needed a job—but he was far too demanding—and good looking to—well, to what? With mixed emotions she moved toward the stove. A fire was already glowing inside the black monster with a kettle of water bubbling merrily atop. Coffee seemed to be perking there as well. Was Roarc up already?

At that moment he entered from the back door carrying a crock of milk. His good morning was brief as he eyed Mylena dressed in a different gown. She was a beauty! He found it difficult to take his eyes off her petite figure with all its curves in just the right places.

"Are you eating breakfast with us this morning?" Mylena moved to pull the granite mixing bowl from the lower cabinet.

"Yes—I thought I would . . . . " His brief answer caused her to sneak a quick look at his handsome face as he deposited the crock on the table. "Thought you might need some more milk."

The quick clatter of footsteps sounded on the loft ladder. Rian, rubbing sleep from his eyes, hopped into the room.

"Did you ask her, Papa? Did you?"

Roarc cleared his throat. "Not yet, son. I was waiting for you." That was a lie he thought to himself. He was a coward when it came to backing down and asking the woman to stay on to work for them. He realized he had been abominably rude when she had arrived earlier in the week before the rainstorm had interrupted negotiations.

"But, Papa, you promised!" Rian was almost crying now.

"Now, son, calm down. We'll ask her." He cleared his throat.

Mylena stopped mixing dough and stared at the pair waiting guiltily side by side and facing her. Would this be the death knell to her staying?

"Rian and I want to know if you would be willing to stay on and work for us. The pay would be twenty dollars a week plus room and board. Would that be satisfactory?"

Mylena could not believe her ears. Stay on? Work for them? What had changed Roarc's mind? Staying was what she had hoped for but . . . . should she give in like a little puppy?

"Well . . . . I . . . . " she began only to be interrupted by Rian.

"Oh please, Miss Mylena. We like you. We want you to stay."

She could no more resist his plea than she could fly out the window. She knelt beside him, put her arms around his small body and answered.

"If that's what you want, I'll stay."

With a whoop he pulled away and began to jump up and down. "She will, Papa! She will!"

"Now calm down, son. That's settled and we need to get on with breakfast."

Mylena turned back to her mixing bowl with a small smile. Roarc Rhynhart was not used to expressing any kind of emotion. This was hard for him.

Breakfast over, Mylena rose to clear the table as Roarc slid his hat atop his dark head.

"If you are staying, we need to show you around the place so you'll know where things are. Will you be ready in about thirty minutes to walk around with Rian and me?"

Surprised, Mylena could only swallow and answer. "Yes I will."

"It's still pretty muddy out so wear something old."

Mylena looked down at her green dress. She didn't really have anything "old" with her.

She had given her old clothes away back in Ohio before she and Will boarded the train for Colorado.

This dress was almost new but it would have to do.

As she hung the dish cloth atop its hanger, Roarc re-entered the kitchen. He held out a pair of rubber boots.

"I found these in the store room. They used to be Lavina's but I think they will just about fit you too. You'll need them for walking around the barn and outbuildings."

Mylena took them only to find them meticulously clean and ready to slip on. Roarc must have spent a while scouring them for her. She stepped out of her shoes and slipped her feet into them. They were a bit too large but they would do nicely.

"Thank you. They will be fine." She grabbed the blanket flung across the rocking chair and wrapped it shawl fashion about her shoulders. "I'm ready."

Rian danced along beside them as they made their way across the back yard. Tall cotton wood trees still dripped a small drop of water now and then as they dodged their icy sting. Under foot the ground was soggy from the rain but not too unpleasant to negotiate.

First they visited the chicken house and pen. Chickens of all types roamed freely about clucking pleasantly as they gobbled up the feed Rian tossed to them.

"You have quite a large flock," Mylena observed.

"It takes a lot of chickens to keep the ranch hands, and us as well, full of fried chicken."

Roarc laughed. He seemed more relaxed outdoors as if this was really his element.

"I see all breeds here. My father always liked Rhode Island Reds because he said they were plump for eating. But my mother wanted White Leghorns for she said they were the best layers."

"Well we have some of both—and some other breeds too. They come in when it's Spring to the post office in Callahan. You should hear all the cheeping then." Roarc laughed again.

"I know. We used to order all of ours as well. Then came the chore of raising them."

A slender white rooster preened himself atop a fence post. Roarc laughed again.

"See that white rooster? He chases Rian every time he catches him out. Rian is deathly afraid of him. That rooster has spurs two inches long and he's a mean one. Watch out for him."

Mylena made a note of this information. No doubt the rooster would be out to test her too. Well, she was certainly used to dealing with chickens so it would be a stand-off.

Next they visited the pig pens. Here two sows wallowed happily in the mud left from the recent rain. Nearby were six piglets squealing as they chased each other about the pen. Rian hung atop the fence giggling as he watched their antics. Soon the smells caused them to move along.

Beyond the corn crib bursting with ears of corn, they entered the huge wooden barn.

Beside the door was a room equipped with a work bench, several stools and sporting a pot bellied stove in one corner. Tools and buckets lined the walls and floor.

"This is where we work when the weather turns bad. We do all our repairs here."

A ladder leading to the loft was next in line. Mylena could see stacks of hay filling the loft. She remembered when her father had been alive and their own barn loft looked like that. But, with her father's death, and Will's taking over the farm, it had never been that way again. Will had just never seemed to get the hang of farming. Will had loved to play his banjo. That had been his real—and only—talent. But Mylena shook her head. She would not think about that now.

She followed Roarc and Rian along the row of stalls—empty now but clean and ready for occupancy. Suddenly Rian made a mad dash into one of them.

"Its Olga, Papa, and she can hardly get up." A black and white bitch panted comfortably in a bed of hay.

"It's time for her pups so don't bother her, son. She knows what she's doing." The mother dog looked ready to pop she was so fat. After a few loving pats, Rian was persuaded to leave her alone and continue down the row of stalls.

The last stall contained a beautiful mare—fat with pregnancy also.

"This is Princess." Rian proceeded to tell Mylena all about the horse. "She is having a foal soon so Papa had her brought in so he could watch her. The sire is Papa's stallion, Arrow."

Roarc rubbed the mare's nose as she stuck her head out of the stall. He produced an apple for her and she snorted happily. Rian laughed in delight. Mylena found herself smiling. She loved horses and this one was a beauty. Apparently Roarc had a knack with animals.

Turning from the row of stalls, they could see several cow hands working in the corral adjoining the barn. Roarc led Mylena and Rian toward them. As one, they all stopped their work and stared at the trio facing them. One older man, small, round, and sporting a gray mustache, came forward. His smile was welcoming.

"Good mornin'. You three are out for an early walk."

Roarc immediately introduced the little man. "This is Mose McClane. He and my Pa were friends. They rode together in the great war. After it was over we all decided to come west and Mose is still with us. He's the right hand man around here. We couldn't do without him."

Mose gave a shy grin declaring, "I really just manage the bunk house and all those honery critters that live there with me." Loud guffaws ricocheted around the yard as five hands walked closer.

"These are our cow hands. They are Sim, Clint, Walt, China and Laredo." All the men doffed their Stetsons and grunted polite "howdys".

"Mrs. Harris, here, will be working for us keeping house, cooking, washing, etc., and mostly teaching Rian to read and cipher."

All the men were polite in their acceptance of the new lady—all except Laredo. Tall, dark and handsome in a lean, mean way, he exuded charm. He had a gleam in his black eyes. Mrs. Harris was some looker! He bet he could bed her within a week. Silently he vowed he would do just that as he eyed her up and down. Any widow he had ever encountered had always seemed ready and willing to take a tumble in the hay with him.

CHAPTER 3

As Mylena finished the dishes the next morning, there was a brisk knock on the back door. Drying her hands quickly, she answered to find Mose standing there with a wide grin on his weathered face.

"It's wash day, Miz Mylena. Do you have things to wash?"

"Indeed I do! Let me gather them up and I'll be right there." She summoned Rian.

"Will you bring me all your dirty clothes—and your Papas' too? Mose says it's wash day so we'll help him—all right?"

Rian was delighted for he always felt important on wash day. It was his job to keep small logs and kindling ready for the fire that would rage beneath the old black wash pot. He dashed back up to the loft and threw down several garments that had seen cleaner days. Mylena even added a few pieces of her own and followed Rian to the wash area in the backyard.

Mose had the wash pot bubbling with hot water and several tubs placed nearby. He was adding some lye soap and stirring with a long stick. Buckets were placed nearby to hold cool water from the well for rinsing the garments. Mylena took one look and decided it was a very workable situation. Rinse water could be used later to water the vegetable garden nearby.

"That tub can be yours," Mose pointed out. "I found the rub board Lavina was supposed to use—but she never did so it's almost like new." He placed the contraption into the hot water in Mylena's tub.

"That's fine," she declared and proceeded to begin washing after adding some soap of her own. White things went in first as she scrubbed up and down on the metal board. Soon she was wringing them out and tossing them into the next tub of cooler water to rinse.

"You'll need more hot water for them britches of Roarc's." Mose added hot water to her tub as he announced this fact. He was correct. The hot water tended to cool quickly in the early morning air. Mylena found herself scrubbing several pairs of pants and several shirts of both Rian and Roarc. Then she added their underwear and finally placed them in the boiling pot to come really clean.

Mose seemed to be washing most of the cow hand's clothes as well.

"That's m'job," he declared when Mylena asked.

"Who usually does Roarc's washing?" Mylena was curious.

"I do—that's why I'm so tickled you're here now." He chuckled at her look of surprise.

"Did Lavina not do it?"

"Nope. Never did. Never did nothing she could get out of." But he didn't add any more and Mylena was reluctant to ask.

Soon they were arranging wet garments along the wire fence behind the house to dry. Mylena had a clothes line in Ohio and she missed having one here. Perhaps Roarc would erect one for her, she murmured to herself as she spread shirts to dry.

Suddenly a dark shadow fell across her side. She turned abruptly and almost collided with Laredo. He wore his hat well back on his dark head and a leering smile on his face.

"Hello, pretty lady. Need some help?" He tossed his cigarette to the ground, stamped it out and reached for another wet garment. He hung it haphazardly on the fence.

"No thank you. I don't need any help." Mylena was cool and pushed the pile of wet garments out of his reach.

"That's okay with me. I'll just watch as you work." His eyes roamed her petite figure as he placed his hands in his pockets and stared. Mylena was embarrassed. Why was he here? Wasn't he supposed to be working in the corrals?

Mose ambled by with a load of wet clothes. "You been assigned to do laundry now?"

With an angry grimace, Laredo answered, "Not hardly, old man. Mind your own business." Mylena was aghast at his rudeness.

Before she could reply, Roarc appeared on the other side of the fence. He was angry.

"Laredo, you are not on wash tub duty! Get back to the corral and get to work!"

The two men eyed each other belligerently. Sparks seemed to arc between them. Finally, Laredo broke his stare and ambled off, hands still in his pockets. Roarc watched him until he disappeared in the door of the barn. Then he shot a quick look at Mylena.

"It's not a good idea to flirt with my men. They don't get much chance to chat up a female so you'd better watch out." He turned and walked swiftly away toward the barn.

Mylena had no time to answer or defend herself. She was not flirting! She was busy doing her job—washing HIS dirty clothes! She got madder by the minute. He was hateful!

Mose came to stand beside her. "Never mind, Missy. Roarc'll get over it. He has a temper but it never lasts long—you'll see."

But Mylena fumed as she finished her work and returned to the house.

Flirting indeed! Hateful man!

Alone in bed that night Mylena allowed herself to cry. She hadn't shed tears since Will's funeral several weeks ago. She had steeled herself to take whatever came next on the chin. But the words Roarc had tossed at her hurt. She had never been a flirt. She had suitors back home in Ohio but they were always circumspect. Jim Toliver at church, Will their next door neighbor, Cyrus the banker's timid son or Sim Reed from the livery stable had all been gentlemen with her. Her father would not have stood for anything less. When he finally encouraged her to marry Will Harris from next door, she had thought long and hard about it. Did she love Will enough to marry him? Her friend, Julie James from the millinery shop, had declared if she had to ask herself that,—she didn't.

But with her father's waning health Mylena knew something had to change. Perhaps Will could take over the farm and life could go on as usual. So—she had agreed to the wedding.

Her father was pleased for he had begun to worry about leaving her alone if something happened to him. Besides she was of marriageable age and girls who waited too long often lost their prospects her father had declared. So—she had agreed.

Their wedding had been simple and their life together dull. Will was a poor lover with little knowledge of how to woo and win a wife. Mylena had often worried that if she herself had been more enthusiastic Will might have been more ardent in the bedroom. The romance novels she and Julie had sneaked to read as young girls described love in a completely different light. Disappointed, Mylena had decided to make the best of a bad bargain and when her father died unexpectedly she was glad she had Will to rely on.

But Will hated farm life. He played the banjo with expertise. A difficult instrument, his skill was recognized far and wide. He was drafted to play for every dance, every gathering for miles around. These were the times he lived for. If he could have made a living playing, his life would have been complete. But there was certainly no monetary value in what he chose to do. Their farm suffered from his ineptness regardless of how hard Mylena tried to help.

In the darkness of her bedroom, her mind wandered back. Will began to read of the promise of new land in Eastern Colorado. Newspapers made the ads of the Colorado land purveyors sound too good to be true. Will succumbed. He began his push to sell the farm and make a move to Colorado. It took him several long months to convince Mylena it was the thing for them to do. Their farm sold quickly. Mylena was glad her father was gone and could never see how it had gone down. Will sent the money to Colorado and was to pick up their deed upon their arrival in Callahan. But Will never made it.

Mylena sat up in the darkness. Memories of the train being set upon by a renegade band of Indians sent chills up her spine. She remembered the plunk of arrows as they hit the walls of their railroad car. The men rallied quickly but they were outnumbered by the savages.

No one knew why they had chosen that day, that train to raid. Perhaps it was for the food being transported on the train. At any rate, they looted the box cars. She could still recall how they had vanished amid whoops of joy. Everyone had declared that must have been it.

Miraculously the engineer had only been wounded and was able to get the train moving on into Callahan. The sheriff there was quick to dispatch help. At least four bodies were recovered inside the Pullman car where Mylena and Will were riding. His was one of them.

Their companions, Mr. and Mrs. Wilson, were moving to Callahan on just such a whim as Will's. But Mr. Wilson was also one of the victims. A young couple caught the additional arrows and died as well. Rumor had it that they were a couple running away to be married. Now no one would ever know.

The town was kind to the two widows. They were given rooms in the town's hotel and visited by members of both churches with offerings of food and much advice. Their husbands were buried in the town's only cemetery along with the missing young couple. However, Mylena noticed the funeral parlor seemed more than pleased to accept full payment for the funeral expenses leaving her little to live on. The sheriff was most accommodating. Mylena didn't ask how many other victims were found at the scene of the raid. She didn't want to know any more about that awful experience.

He visited them at the hotel suggesting they apply for jobs in the area. The local doctor was looking for a lady to act as his nurse and keep his records. A local rancher was seeking someone to become his housekeeper and help care for his five-year old son. After much discussion, the two women agreed and let it be known they were available.

The doctor immediately chose Mrs. Wilson for she had been a doctor's daughter and was somewhat familiar with what he would need. That left Mylena with the rancher's job. Sheriff Rollins sent a runner to Roarc Rhynhart's ranch with news that he had a lady just right for his job. Mr. Rhynhart sent back word that he would be pleased to have her. But upon her arrival there, Mr. Rhynhart had voiced his opinion of her in no uncertain terms. But here she still was . . . . and he had insinuated she was a "flirt".

Still angry, she lay back down but it was a long time before she fell asleep.

Up in the loft Roarc was doing some soul-searching of his own. He really should not have accused Mylena of being a flirt. He hadn't meant to. She had been nothing but a lady since her arrival. He knew Laredo. He fancied himself a ladies' man and had caused several ruckuses when he went to town on Saturday night.

Roarc turned on his other side as Rian slept peacefully beside him. Roarc could see the moon shining in the end of the loft. Cooler weather would arrive in the fall and it would be too cold to sleep up here. He'd better be thinking of some way to alleviate that little problem.

But every time he closed his eyes a vision of Mylena intruded—her big blue eyes, the wisps of dark curls that drifted across her cheeks while she worked in the kitchen, the tiny waist that he bet his hands could span—and the curves they accented even through the fabric of her dress. He had spied her ankles. He wondered if her legs were as shapely . . . . he turned on his other side. He HAD to get some sleep!

Mylena overslept. By the time she was washed and dressed in a clean pink patterned dress, Roarc had disappeared. The stove was glowing and a pot of coffee simmered there. An empty tin cup rested in the sink bearing testimony that he had been there earlier. She could hear Rian rustling about in the loft and he soon appeared.

"What's for breakfast, Miss Mylena? I'm hungry!"

"You are a bottomless pit, young man," she laughed as she pulled out the iron skillet ready to make bacon and scrambled eggs.

As they ate, Roarc came through the back door. He doffed his Stetson and said good morning to both of them. Then he proceeded to move on across the room to his battered desk in the opposite corner. There he shuffled some papers, stuffed some of them in his shirt pocket and came back by the table.

"Would you like some breakfast?" Mylena asked as if she weren't still angry enough to kick his shins.

"No, I ate with the boys in the bunk house. We've been talking. I think we'll enclose the wall between your bedroom and the storage room and make another bedroom for Rian and me. This winter it will be too cold to sleep in the loft even if I finish enclosing it—and I'll do that too."

He shifted on one boot, then the other. Seemed like Mylena was still miffed at him. Well, he didn't blame her—but be switched if he would apologize. She needed to stay away from Laredo!

"Mose and I will be taking the wagon into town on Saturday to pick up some lumber.

Do you need supplies?"

"Can I go too, Papa?" Rian was immediately alert to a trip to town.

"I don't see why not. How about you, Mrs. Harris, do you want to go?"

"Yes I would like to. There are a few things I need. Do you want me to make up a list of food we need? "

"That would be fine. We'll leave right after breakfast so we'll have plenty of time to shop and be home before dark."

With that he breezed out the door whistling softly as he went. He had things to do. Besides maybe she would be in a better humor with him now if she had a trip to town to look forward to. That had always seemed to please Lavina—and Mrs. Harris—er—Mylena—was a woman too.

CHAPTER 4

"Miss Mylena! Come quick! Olga had her pups!" Rian was breathless as he scooted to a stop in the kitchen door. "Wanta see 'em?"

"Sure I do. Let's go!" She followed the little boy from the back porch and across the yard toward the barn.

But they were not the only ones out for a morning stroll. The young White Leghorn rooster was also out on patrol. He was feeling particularly frisky this morning. He spied Rian and headed for him spurs aquiver. Rian was just the right size to catch his attention.

Before Rian knew it, the feathered fiend was attacking his ankles. Rian let out a wild scream as he ran away. Mylena picked up a rock and threw it with all her might at the nasty little monster. But she missed. Flapping her skirt at him, and stomping her feet, she finally made him back away and strut off.

"That rooster is a menace. He should be in the Sunday stew pot!"

"But we can't eat him. Papa wants a young, new rooster 'cause Ole Red is getting old."

"Well, we'll see!" Mylena had generated a decided dislike for the feisty fowl.

Entering the barn, the rooster episode was forgotten as Rian headed for the empty stall Olga had made her own. Bedded in a swath of hay, she lay nursing seven tiny puppies.

"See 'em. There's seven of 'em." Rian was ecstatic. "Papa says not to touch 'em yet but Olga won't mind. She knows I'll love 'em." He ran a small finger along one pup's slick back. Olga raised her head, sniffed his hand and wagged her tail as if to agree with him.

Mose came by as they admired the litter.

"Sure gonna have a lot of dogs to get rid of one of these days . . . . " he began but Rian's eyes filled with tears.

"Don't talk about that, Mose. They're just babies now."

Mose ruffled Rian's tawny hair. "I know, boy. That's a long way off."

Talk at the table that night was all about Olga and her babies. That is until Roarc asked Mylena if she had her list made out. She did. She reached across the end of the table and handed him the handwritten list of items she thought they needed.

"If that's too much, I can pare it down some."

"No, it looks good to me. We buy flour and sugar in barrels and sometimes molasses.

We'll see what Mr. Dickens has on hand Saturday."

Saturday couldn't come too soon for Mylena. She looked forward to a trip to town with animation. Maybe, with a bit of relaxation, she would feel better next week about this job.

Mylena spent the afternoon rummaging inside the storage room. She found several treasures. First of all, she discovered four flat irons plus the handle. Next she unearthed an ironing board dirty but repairable. And her final find was the metal bathtub with a tall back—ideal for a woman. This must have been Lavina's. It was dusty but she dragged it out into the kitchen and began the chore of cleaning all her finds.

After cleaning and polishing the flat irons, she re-covered the ironing board with one of the largest dish cloths. She had to retrieve her sewing basket from her trunk but she soon had the cloth stitched together tightly to make an ideal board for ironing. Just to try them out, she set the board across two chair backs while the irons heated atop the stove. When she judged them to be ready, she attached the handle to one iron and tried it out on a shirt spread across the clean board. It worked.

Before many minutes had passed, she exchanged the cooling iron for a hot one and continued ironing. She hung each shirt on a chair and wondered where she should put them away.

Luckily Rian chose that time to come in from play.

"Where should I put these clean shirts?" She indicated her work as she put the irons and ironing board away in the storage room once more.

"We always had them in the drawers of the bedroom. Papa emptied them when you were coming . . . . so I don't know."

Mylena went swiftly to the chest in her bedroom. Sure enough two drawers were still empty as she had never unpacked her trunk. She gently folded the clean, pressed shirts and laid them in the empty drawers. There was no need to disrupt the household just because she was here.

Suppertime found them gathered about the table enjoying a stew she had concocted earlier in the day. As Roarc laid down his spoon and scooted his chair back from the table, Mylena announced.

"Tonight is bath night. I found a bath tub today in the storage room. Where do you suggest I put it for a bath?"

"But Papa and me always take a bath at the bunk house. Why do you need a bath tub in here?" Rian was curiosity itself.

"Because ladies don't bathe in the bunk house, son. We'll carry the tub into your bedroom, Mylena, and fill it with hot water while you finish up the dishes. How about that?" Roarc seemed to fit easily into this idea.

Mylena sat back in the tub with a smile on her face. It was heavenly to soak in a tub of warm water after spending so long in the storage room amid dust and spider webs. She had packed several bars of her favorite soap before leaving Ohio so, with one of them unearthed, she sponged her ivory body in delight. She could even wash her hair and did so quickly.

Wrapped in a robe of flannel, she was brushing out her long hair when a knock rattled her bedroom door. That was Roarc's knock, she would know it anywhere.

"Yes? What?" she called.

"Rian and I are going to the bunk house to bathe. Do you want me to empty your bath water before we go?"

"Yes, please." She opened her door to admit the pair, then stood watching them as they made away with the tub of cooling water. They would pour it on the garden she was sure before they tuned the tub upside down on the back porch.

Alone in the house, she moved out into the main room and stood before the fireplace embers to dry her long swath of hair. Little known to her, Roarc came to the back door, saw her standing there and stopped immediately. He was mesmerized as she stroked her hair brush through the long tresses as he watched. He felt a sizzle of awareness. This would never do! He turned away in disgust. He was not looking for another woman in his life! Swiftly he made his way to the bunk house where Mose already had Rian immersed in a tub of soapy water as the little boy laughed in glee at Mose's antics with the soap and wash cloth.

Breakfast consisted of steaming bowls of oatmeal the following morning. They were in a rush to leave for town. Mylena had not made biscuits but toasted some muffins she had made earlier in the week. She was surprised she still had some left over.

At last it was time to board the wagon Mose had hitched and waiting at the front yard.

Mylena had pondered what to wear. The townspeople would probably wonder if she didn't wear black as they probably still thought of her as a widow. But she didn't have anything black to wear. She had borrowed a black veil from Louise Wilson to wear to the funerals so many weeks ago now.

She shook out a dark blue skirt and jacket. That would have to do. Adding her white blouse, she felt quite dressed up for a change. She added a tiny hat that didn't seem too crushed from its stay in the trunk tray. She had put her hair up so the wind would not blow her into disarray.

She grabbed her tiny hand bag and stepped briskly to the front door where Roarc was waiting.

He closed and locked the door behind her. Then he turned holding out his hand to her.

"Here's your wages for the first two weeks. You might need money today."

"Oh, thank you!" Mylena was impressed with his thoughtfulness. She WOULD need some money when she got to town. She had several chores to take care of.

Rian and Mose rode in the wagon bed on their way to town. Mylena sat beside Roarc in the wagon seat as they rolled along the dirt road to Callahan. Although she tried to keep her distance, an occasional bounce of the wagon jostled her and she bumped her shoulder against his or brushed his thigh with hers as they rode along. Roarc seemed impervious to this as he guided the team.

After several miles of silence between the two, he glanced at her.

"Do you think you'll go back to Ohio?"

Startled, Mylena shot a quick glance at him. "Well—I haven't really had time to think about it. Probably not. My mother and father are both gone now. My brother Ned was killed at Shiloh during he war. Now Will is no longer around and we sold the farm so—I really have very little to return for."

"What about friends?" Roarc couldn't restrain his curiosity.

"Sure, I have some friends there—but they have lives of their own. What would I do there now?"

"Hmm. Good question." Roarc seemed to smile as he flipped the reins atop the horses.

"Papa, I see town!" Rian jumped up pointing to the silhouette of buildings in the distance. Several windmills, a church steeple and the railroad depot loomed in sight.

"Sit down, son. I see it. I don't want you to fall out of the wagon now. Sit down!"

Mose restrained the little boy as they all looked forward in anticipation.

"Where do you want to go first?" he asked Mylena. He slowed the team as they approached the wide street lined on both sides with wooden buildings. Most of them boasted two stories with only a few smaller edifices in between.

"The hotel I think. I still have some things stored there. I need to see about them."

"Anything that needs to go back to the ranch?"

"No. These are Will's things. I'm not sure what I'll do with them."

Roarc pulled the team to a standstill before the hotel door. He jumped from the wagon and moved quickly around to help Mylena down. She paused searching for the foothold. Swiftly Roarc raised his brawny arms and placed his hands about her tiny waist lifting her to the ground easily.

Breathless, Mylena could only thank him and shake out her skirts from the long ride.

"Let's meet at the hotel dining room at three o'clock. Will that give you enough time to take care of everything?" Roarc scanned her face as he made this suggestion.

"Yes, that will be fine. Thanks." Mylena turned away to enter the hotel as Roarc watched her retreating back—slim, supple, curvy. He stopped himself immediately. But he had guessed his hands could span her waist—and they could. He smiled in satisfaction as he flipped the reins and guided the wagon toward the lumber mill.

"Well, hello, dearie. We wondered if we'd ever see you again." The strident voice of the hotel manager's wife assailed Mylena's ears as she entered the hotel door. Nora Davis and her husband, Dan, ran the hotel. A least Dan Davis was advertised as the manager. In fact he was simply a stooge for his over-bearing wife Nora who really ruled the roost with a fist of iron.

Mylena smiled as she advanced toward the check-in counter.

"I came to see about the things I left here in storage. I need to do something with them."

"Oh? What do you plan to do?" Nora's curiosity was rampant. She had already picked the lock on the trunk and delved clear to the bottom to see just what was inside. The other case held a banjo—well-used but still in tune.

"I'm not sure. What do you suggest?" Mylena was suspicious of the woman and wanted her input before she committed herself in any way. This was a bit like the games of poker she used to play with her brother when their parents weren't looking. Bluffs sometimes worked wonders.

"Do you want to sell it all?" Nora knew what was there—clothing, shaving supplies of razor, strop, mug and brush. There were several packets of old pictures which would never sell but the other things certainly would. She might even find someone who could play that silly banjo too. Nora grabbed a key to the storage room and led the way as Mylena followed.

Mylena opened the trunk with her own key, then scanned the contents. Will's clothing brought a tear to her eye and his shaving supplies made them fall for a moment. She could never use these things again. She might as well sell them—even Will's banjo—especially Will's banjo. She never wanted to hear a note again.

Mylena turned to Nora suddenly. "How much for the whole lot?"

Nora, acting innocent, suggested a low figure. She could certainly make some money on the side selling these things after Mylena went back to the ranch. But Mylena didn't agree.

"No, I'll need more than that. All these clothes are practically new and, being from back east they are of good quality. I couldn't take less than fifty dollars for the trunk and ten more for the banjo."

Nora quickly calculated these figures. Too high—but the girl was right. The things were of good quality and Nora could make some money on them even at that rate. She nodded in agreement and led the way back to the check-in desk. There she handed Mylena the money and held out her hand for the trunk key. With a few more words, Mylena left the hotel—forever she hoped!

The doctor's office was directly across from the hotel. Mylena looked both ways for horse traffic before she crossed the street. Grasping the metal door knob, she swung the office door inward to spy Louise Wilson diligently writing in a file. Waiting a few moments, she finally cleared her throat to attract Louise's attention.

"Mylena! My lands! Get in here!" Louise rose to embrace the younger woman immediately. "Where did you come from?"

Mylena went on to explain her presence in town today. Louise suggested a cup of tea and Mylena agreed with alacrity. Soon they were sipping the fragrant brew as Louise asked all about the ranch and her job.

"The job is going all right. The little boy, Rian, is a joy and very well-behaved. The house is adequate with an indoor water pump and an enormous fireplace."

"What about the rancher—the boss?"

Mylena felt her face growing hot. "The boss? Well—he's a bit overbearing and not too easy to deal with." Now was that fair? He had been nothing but accommodating—except for calling her a "flirt". She lowered her eyes and stirred her tea slowly.

"Umhm. Sounds interesting." Louise had a twinkle in her eye as she watched the younger woman with interest.

A loud shout interrupted their visit. The door banged open and two men carried another into the room. The victim's leg was bloody and he was grimacing in severe pain.

"Whatever has happened?" Louise was immediately on her feet and bustling about.

"Jake here cut his leg chopping wood. Is the doc in?"

"He is—and I'll call him right now." Louise bustled off to do just that. Soon she was returning with the doctor who took over the care of the injured man and escorted him into an inner office. Louise followed with a wave of her hand.

Mylena felt it was time for her to go. Louise was doing fine.

Strolling along the boardwalk, she met Mose and Rian.

"Lookee, Miss Mylena, Mose bought me a peppermint stick." He waved the sweet candy cane in the air.

"Everything going all right?" Mose eyed Mylena with interest. She seemed to be having a good time.

"Yes, I'm on my way to the mercantile. I have a bit of shopping to do now."

With a wave she was soon down the street and entering the mercantile where goods of all descriptions were stacked on tables or lined up in shelves.

Some were even displayed in baskets on the floor. Mylena was entranced. It had been a while since she went shopping just for the fun of it.

When she had been here previously she had been in the throes of burying her dead husband and trying to make a decision about what to do with her life next.

She fingered rolls of calico but she really didn't need any new dresses. She touched the yardages of lace and picked up some spools of thread she might need. She selected two hanks of knitting yarn to make an afghan. Her knitting needles and crochet hooks were in her trunk waiting to be used once more. She moved to the racks displaying books. There were a few she could use to teach Rian the alphabet and his numbers. She added these to her shopping basket.

Before she knew it, it was time to meet the others at the hotel dining room. She paid for her purchases and turned to leave the store. Mose and Rian met her at the door.

"We was just comin' to find you, Missy. It's time to eat." Mose propelled her toward the cafe as Rian trotted along beside him.

Upon entering the large room, Roarc rose from a seat at a table near the front windows.

He noticed Mylena's packages with a raised eyebrow.

"I see you HAVE been shopping." His white smile belied his teasing words.

"Yes. It's been very nice to be in town once more. I've enjoyed it." Mylena draped her napkin across her lap as the waitress came to take their order.

"What's the special for the day?" Roarc asked as she handed them a sheet of paper bearing the menu list.

"Chicken and dumplin's, sir." she answered with a smile. No female could resist Roarc's smile mused Mylena sourly to herself. She, herself, didn't seem immune to it.

"I'll have that—and the boy will have a half order."

"But, Papa, I'm hungry!" pouted Rian with a disappointed look on his small face.

"I know—and you'll want a slice of chocolate pie too so you'd better leave room for that, remember?"

Rian's face broke into a sunny smile. "Yeah. I remember."

Mose and Mylena agreed with the order and soon they were sampling the delicious offerings of the town's main cafe.

Two of Roarc's cow hands ambled from the rear of the room and stopped by their table.

"I hear there's a big celebration going on near the depot. It seems the railroad has been finished all the way to Colorado Springs and they're marking the day." Clint was full of this news.

"There's music and dancing and speeches. Think we'll hang around to see what it's all about."

"Thanks for telling us. We may want to check it out too." Roarc pulled out his wallet in preparation of their leaving. But Mylena placed a hand on his arm.

"I'm paying for my own dinner."

Outraged, Roarc declared, "You are not!. This is my treat. I invited you. Besides I'm paying for Mose and Rian too. So, lady, that's the end of it." His devastating smile softened his words causing Mylena to subside with a quiet "thank you".

Once outside the building, they could hear music in the air. Mose and Rian were definitely interested in seeing what the commotion was all about. Roarc asked if they all wanted to go to the depot to see what was happening. This resulted in agreeable nods all around. There was quite a crowd surrounding the yellow wooden building adjacent to the railroad tracks. A steam engine puffed softly as if waiting to depart. There was a bandstand and a small dance floor constructed near the depot itself. Speeches were being made relating to the newly completed railroad on to Colorado Springs some forty miles away.

Clapping for the final speech ended and the band struck up a lively tune for dancing.

Several couples moved onto the floor and began their graceful gyrations. Mylena followed Mose and Rian as they walked closer to the dance floor to watch. Roarc found some of his friends leaning against a tree so he stopped to talk with them. Mose tapped his feet to the music and grinned in delight. If there was anything he enjoyed, it was a good dance with a purty gal.

The next tune was to "Put your Little Foot". He could stand it no longer. He grabbed Mylena's hand and dragged her to the dance floor.

"You know this one, gal. I know you do. Let's go!"

Fortunately she did know it. It had been a favorite back home in Ohio. She had often danced it with someone while Will played his banjo. Will had never cared for dancing—just the music.

Now Mose guided her in the twirly steps. He was an expert making it easy for her to follow. Rian stood at the edge of the floor with a wide grin on his face. Looked like fun to him. Roarc watched too—but from farther away—and surreptitiously.

Breathless and laughing at the end of the dance, Mylena was shocked when Laredo grabbed her and swung her around pulling her close to his wiry body. He smelled of liquor and cigarettes causing Mylena to cough. Before she could utter a word, the music began again and he whirled her away in a fast stepping pace.

She tried to pull away to catch her breath but he held her even closer. She could barely move and she could feel every muscle of his body boring into hers. He swung her about, then pulled her back close in his arms until she became a bit dizzy. It was a miserable dance. She thought the music would never end. Fortunately, at last, it did but Laredo didn't release her. He began to whisper in her ear.

"Let's you and me ditch this dance, darlin'. I know a place to go you'll like more than this . . . . "

Abruptly Mylena felt her arm held in a strong hand and she was tugged from Laredo's clasp.

"Sorry, buddy, but this next dance is mine." It was Roarc. He hadn't intended to dance at all but he couldn't stand watching what Laredo was doing to Mylena. He HAD to intervene. Now he swung her away in a slow waltz and she relaxed thankfully as she followed his steps easily.

"I wasn't flirting," she blurted for his ears alone.

He grinned self-consciously. "I know. I'm sorry about that." Then he pulled her just a mite closer as he turned along the floor.

When the dance was over, he held her hand as they exited the dance floor quickly.

"I think it's time for us to go. Laredo is liquored up and I'm sure he may try to cause some trouble. I don't want a fight and I don't want to go to jail tonight so—let's go while we can. It will be just about dark when we get home now."

Mose had watched the proceedings and nodded his agreement. Mylena and Rian walked swiftly beside the men as they headed for the wagon parked on the street.

This time the wagon was so loaded they all had to ride on the wagon seat. It was crowded but they squeezed in. Rian sat in Mose's lap as the back of the wagon was covered with a tarp and bore a bumpy silhouette beneath its cover. Mylena was wedged between Mose's lumpy shoulder and

Roarc's hard muscled arm and thigh. They all talked of their day in town but home looked mighty good when they got there. Rian was half asleep so Roarc took him from Mose, helped Mylena down with his other hand and asked Mose to unhitch the horses. They would leave the loaded wagon in the barn yard until morning.

CHAPTER 5

Morning found the entire group unloading the wagon. Mylena gathered her packages with care but stood watching as the men continued removing items from the wagon bed. Roarc reached in, then set a new rocking chair on the ground. Startled, Mylena could only rub the satiny wood and exclaim at its beauty.

"But, Roarc, you already have a rocker. Why a new one?"

"I notice you sit in a straight chair while I read Rian's Bible story at night so I thought you might like a rocker of your own."

Touched by his thoughtfulness, Mylena felt her eyes fill with unshed tears. She could only whisper a soft "thank you" in return. Roarc asked where she wanted to put it. She turned to lead the way to the house and indicate the space opposite his rocker before the fireplace. Still amazed at his action, she raised swimming eyes to him. He stopped, placed a bronzed hand beneath her chin and teased, "We aim to keep our lady comfortable here."

The moment shattered into laughter as he turned to retrace his steps to the barn where the action was. Mylena sat down gingerly in the new rocker. She smiled softly to herself as she rocked with pleasure.

All hands were drafted to help in building the new bedroom. Two of them laid timbers for the flooring, two more began joining the roof overhead. Roarc knew exactly what he wanted and supervised every facet of the work. Rian was generally in the way until Mose undertook his supervision by directing him to help in the barn where Olga's pups were growing by leaps and bounds. Rian could hold each of them now and pet them to his heart's content.

Mylena kept busy inside the house and out of the way. She was baking loaves of bread and the aroma gave the hands much needed pleasure as they worked.

Laredo seemed to be everywhere she went. His dark eyes held a knowing glow as if he had a secret she didn't know about. She was afraid she did know what he was thinking. After all, she had been married. She knew.

Roarc kept a sharp eye on the man. He didn' t trust him near Mylena at all. Last year Laredo had been arrested in town for molesting a bar maid. He had been jailed for several days until Roarc had finally intervened and vouched for him to the tune of fifty dollars. Laredo was a good worker, especially with the horses.

At the end of the day Mose and Roarc sat on the front porch sipping a last cup of coffee.

"I see you watching Laredo. What you gonna do about him?" Mose didn't like the man.

"Don't know, Mose. He's a good worker and I hate to lose him for that—but. I can't trust him around women. I'm concerned for Mylena's safety. I'm afraid if I let him go, he will just hang around and cause more trouble. I would have no authority over him then. I don't know what to do."

"Well time will tell," Mose consoled in a low voice.

Mylena loved working with the chickens. One hen seemed to take a liking to her as well. "Miz Red" Mylena called her laughingly. The chicken would even eat out of Mylena's hand and follow her about. But the little white rooster continued to be a pest. Both Mylena and Rian had to watch out for him when they were in the yard.

One day they were coming from the hen house where they had been gathering eggs for Mylena to make a custard pudding. The rooster suddenly swooped down on them with spurs shining.

Mylena spied a piece of wire on the ground. She reached down, grabbed the wire and slung it at the offending rooster. The wire spiraled around his neck and spun him in an arc through the air. He landed with a kerplunk on the ground nearby. He lay still as death.

Mylena put a hand to her mouth. Had she killed him? She certainly hadn't meant to!

Rian, round-eyed, declared, "Papa will be mad. You killed his new rooster. We better bury him right quick." Actually Rian was happy to be rid of his nemesis.

"No, we'll just leave him there until I tell your Pa." Mylena herded Rian on to the house with a heavy heart. She hated that little white monster but she hadn't meant to kill him outright.

Both Rian and Mylena were unusually quiet at the noon meal. Roarc wondered what had caused their subdued silence—but he didn't ask. He was far too busy finishing up the new bedroom to bother with their problems right now.

"Good meal, Mylena. Custard pudding is my favorite. Well, it's back to work." He was gone. Mylena breathed a sigh of relief.

"You didn't tell him," Rian accused in a small voice.

"I know. I'm a coward. I just couldn't!" She began gathering up their dirty dishes and placing them in a pan of hot water. "I'll tell him tonight, I promise."

Much later in the afternoon Mylena was cleaning out the fireplace readying it for a new batch of kindling when Rian came bursting in the back door.

"Miss Mylena! Come quick!"

Alarmed, she rose to grab the puffing little boy as he ground to a stop beside her.

"You gotta see this! It's the rooster!"

"What?" So—someone had discovered the deed she had done. Well, she was in for it now. She followed Rian slowly as he ran back outside.

"See?" He pointed a grubby little finger at the white rooster walking slowly and shaking his head. "He's not dead after all."

Mylena stared in unbelief. She hadn't killed Roarc's rooster. She had simply stunned him. She placed both hands to her throat and smiled. What a reprieve.

The day finally came when the men cut the door into the new bedroom. Adjacent to the fireplace, and next to the storage room, the new door opened up much needed space in the house. Two of the cow hands spent most of the day white washing the walls while Mylena polished the window panes. At the close of the day, Roarc broke out a bottle of homemade wine to celebrate.

"We made quick work of this job, boys. I congratulate you." He poured tin mugs of the dark liquid and raised his own in a toast. Amid much laughter and back slapping, the entire crew came in for his expression of appreciation. Mose became quite loquacious while the others nudged each other in the ribs and grinned.

"Mose never could hold his liquor," murmured Laredo in a jeering stage whisper.

Fortunately Roarc didn't hear this remark. He was too busy steering Mose back to the bunk house.

The next morning Roarc took a look round the new room, then came out to the kitchen to announce. "I know it isn't Saturday but I think I'll hitch up the wagon and go into town to find a new bedstead and mattress or feather bed—whatever Mr. Dickens has in stock."

Mylena turned and clasped her hands in front of her. She wore a serious look on her face. Would Roarc be agreeable?

"May I talk to you a minute?"

Roarc felt a cold chill race over him. She wanted to leave. What could he say? He didn't want her to leave! How could they keep her here?

He swallowed the lump forming in his throat. "Sure." He propped a hip against the dining table and prepared for trouble.

"Well—I was just thinking about something. You know the chest in my bedroom is so big—too big really for just my things. Your clothes and Rian's fit nicely in it too. Why don't you move it into the new bedroom? I have some money from the things I sold Nora Davis so I would like to buy a small dresser with a larger mirror." Would he agree?

Roarc grinned in relief She wasn't asking to leave after all.

"A larger mirror you say? Typical female!" He laughed. "I don't see that as a problem. Do you want to go see about finding one today?"

It was as if sunshine broke over Mylena's face. Her smile made a sizzle zip through Roarc as he watched her rosy lips widen in a merry smile.

"Oh I would! When?"

"Well—let's go now." He was amazed at how good it felt to please her—to bring such a happy smile to her pretty face.

"Now? Well—that's fine with me . . . . " She began to snatch off the dish towel she used as an apron and run a hand over her hair pinned up today for coolness. "What about Rian?"

"Oh I'm sure he'll want to go too. He never forgets the candy available in Dicken's store.

I'll see about the wagon right away and tell Mose."

Mylena stood for long minutes savoring such a pleasant interlude with the autocratic Roarc. Or was he? Maybe it was just his good looks that kept her at a distance. There had been no unpleasant instances in weeks now. She turned at last toward her bedroom with a decision to make as to what to wear for a day in town shopping.

The wagon jostled along the uneven road as Mylena attempted to keep her umbrella upright for shade. Rian sat between them and chattered all the way. It seemed forever before they spied the town's buildings in the distance. White puffs of clouds drifted lazily across the sky. Mylena found herself feeling happy for the first time in months. She no longer had her father's farm to worry about—it was sold. She didn't have Will to worry about—then she felt almost guilty. Of course she wasn't glad he had been killed! She stopped her thoughts immediately and turned to Rian.

"We're going to visit Mr. Dickens so you need to stay with us today."

"Can I have some candy?" Rian smiled a sunny grin as she nodded in agreement.

Inside Mr. Dickens store, he eyed them with speculation. Here they were buying furniture together. Were they getting married? Or were they just sleeping in the same bed?

Mylena found her dresser quickly. She knew what she wanted—something like she had owned back home in Ohio—and she found one. It was moderately priced too so she came away smiling.

It took Roarc and Rian longer to make up their minds about a bedstead and mattress.

They seemed to be the ones trying out mattresses so Mr. Dickens revised his thoughts. Mylena went back inside the mercantile while the two Rhynharts made their decision about a mattress.

The ride home was a merry one. Their shopping had gone well. Roarc had found a new iron bedstead and a mattress new to the market. He had even bought an armless chair for the new bedroom. Mylena had found just the dresser she had dreamed of. Mr. Dickens had furniture shipped in by railroad now and then. They had caught him with a good supply.

Mylena didn't have time to visit Louise Wilson as, after a meal at the hotel dining room, they began their journey home once more. Roarc hoped to set up the new furniture before dark.

He braked the wagon in the front yard. Three of the cow hands were lounging beside the bunk house after supper. They came forward as he motioned for them to help him unload.

"We barely made it home before the sun went down but, with a little work, we'll be unloaded and set up by bedtime."

Thankfully Rian needed to go see about Olga and her pups so he was out of the way which was a blessing. With tugs and grunts the big chest of drawers was moved into the new bedroom.

Next Mylena's new dresser was set up in her room. She was busy cleaning the mirror almost before the men set it down.

Mose ambled in to say he had a big pot of chili left over and ready in the bunk house. Roarc and Rian washed up and joined him there but Mylena had no desire for such hot food tonight. She was much too busy sorting clothing and arranging the new dresser drawers. She finally unpacked her trunk.

Perhaps she would be staying a while after all.

CHAPTER 6

It was a halcyon time in the middle of summer. The stock was grazing on the long grass fattening for fall sales. The crops were bursting with growth that would result in a bountiful harvest.

But now the garden produce was at its highest. Mose had declared it was time to put up some green beans as the vines were loaded. Tomorrow, early, they would begin that chore.

Mylena listened as Roarc read Rian a Bible story before bed. The night was warm so she stepped out onto the front porch where she leaned against a porch post to savor the cool night breeze. A full moon was rising in the east casting a molten glow over the landscape. Stars twinkled in a black velvet sky as she sat down on the top step of the porch to enjoy the view. She could hear Roarc leading Rian up to bed in the loft. It was still much cooler up there for sleeping in mid-summer.

She sat on longing silently for something—she didn't know what. She couldn't put a finger to it.

Suddenly Roarc spoke from behind her. He was leaning against a porch post in the moonlight filling a pipe. He shook out a match and sent a puff of aromatic smoke into the air.

Mylena glanced up. "I didn't know you smoked."

"I don't usually. Once in a great while I enjoy a pipe. I never liked cigarettes. Besides I don't have time to smoke. I'm usually too busy." His soft chuckle filled the air.

"It's a beautiful night." Mylena was at a loss for words. They had never shared much conversation except when riding in the wagon to town and back. Then there was usually someone else along to chime in.

"It is," he sat down beside her on the top porch step. A spirit of camaraderie seemed to envelope them as they sat there in the pale light. He propped his arms on his knees and puffed peacefully.

"Does this remind you of Ohio?" He shot a glance at her perfect profile.

"Oh no. There are a lot of trees in Ohio. The fields are smaller and bounded by rows of trees. It's nothing like this."

"Do you miss it?"

"I really haven't had time to miss it. This country is different and needs some getting used to I guess."

"My wife never got used to it." He puffed contentedly on his pipe.

"Never?" Mylena was astounded that he would mention his wife. He never had before.

"No, never. She hated it."

"But why? You were beginning a new life here—why not like it?"

"She had been raised by a family with several slaves back in Missouri. She had never had to do much for herself—and she never got used to doing without them."

"I'm sorry," Mylena shot a quick glance at his profile in the moonlight. With all they had here—and being married to a virile man like Roarc—she couldn't imagine being unhappy.

"Was she happy with her baby?"

"Not really. She never wanted a child to take care of—and she didn't. The last two months before Rian was born she spent in town in the home of the doctor and his wife who was still living then. They doted on Lavina and cosseted her. She enjoyed that. We were worried about the actual childbirth but she sailed right through that with no problem. We were worried that the baby would be sickly—but Rian has always been the picture of health. That is a blessing."

"Yes. But then what happened to her?"

"When Rian was three we had an exceptionally bad winter. Lavina took a bad cold. It turned into pneumonia and we lost her. My Pa did the same thing. We lost both of them within a month."

"How awful for you." Mylena felt tears fill her eyes.

"It was hard but Mose is a great help. Without him I would have been lost I guess."

Mylena felt a lump in her throat at the sadness in his voice. But he turned to her with some questions of his own.

"Tell me about Will. Do you still miss him?"

"Will?" The sudden change of topic surprised her. "Well—yes I miss him. He was like a big brother to me. He grew up on the farm next door and he was just always there. We went to school together, to church, to everything that went on in our area. His one love in life was playing his banjo."

"How come you sold the farm there?"

"Will was just never a farmer. He was the youngest of five boys. The older brothers did the farming while he played his music. When we married and he came to our farm my father thought things would be fine. But they weren't. Will just couldn't get the hang of farming and things went down. My father saw this before he died but it was too late then. After he died, Will talked me into selling. I thought we might as well."

"Was he good with his gun then?"

"Never. Poor Will. He was as likely to drop his gun when he drew it as he was to fire it.

His brothers teased him often about that."

"Were you in love with Will?" Curiosity killed the cat, mused Roarc

"In love? I'm not sure I know what that means . . . . " Mylena looked down at her hands in the moonlight and found them shaking. She shouldn't be having this talk with this man. He was too handsome, too virile, too . . . everything.

She rose to end their shared intimacy. He stood as well. Mylena was so close to him she could feel his smoky breath—smell his outdoor scent—sense the warmth of his hard body close to her. What would it feel like to be held in his hard arms, to lay her head against his broad shoulder?

With a quick shake of her head, she murmured "Goodnight." She almost ran to her bedroom and shut the door. She leaned against it for long moments. What was wrong with her? She had never reacted to a man like this before!

Roarc stood still as a statue for several seconds after she disappeared. Then he knocked the cold ash from his pipe and made his way up the loft ladder to his bed. He lay with his arms behind his dark head just thinking of all the things she had told him. She sounded completely unawakened to the ways of love.

Daylight found Mose rapping on the back door and rattling buckets. Mylena opened sleepy eyes and remembered they were picking green beans today. She had better get up and get busy.

Roarc and Rian came down from the loft as she filled the coffeepot with water. Apparently Mose had awakened everyone today.

"We need to pick them beans while it's cool." Mose led the way as Mylena grabbed her bonnet and followed him to the bean patch.

Plump and ready, the beans mounded as Mose dumped them into tubs to be washed and sorted. Mylena was almost finished picking the last row as she looked up to find a pair of boots blocking her way. Startled, she lifted her eyes up—up—up. Laredo stood there. His mocking smile and leering eyes always alarmed her. She rose slowly, bucket in hand.

"Hello, pretty lady. The boss is busy in the barn so I thought you might need some help picking beans."

"No, we're almost finished." Mylena blurted as Mose disappeared around the corner of the house for some reason. Now she was alone with this man who frightened her.

"Well let me help you with that . . . . " He reached for her shoulder and pulled her toward his wiry body. Mylena pushed at him and screamed. He grabbed her and planted a smoky kiss on her mouth. Releasing her with a grin, he whispered, "You and me could make some beautiful music together, lady. How about it?"

Mylena screamed, "No!" and threw the bucket of beans at him. Green beans covered him from head to toe as curses emanated from his spitting mouth.

Sudden fury burst on the scene as Roarc grabbed the unwary cow hand and spun him in an arc. His hard fist landed in the middle of Laredo's face as blood spurted from his nose.

"You bastard! You are fired. You get off this ranch and stay off. We don't manhandle our women here." Roarc was more than angry—he was furious.

"Oh—is she your little dolly-bird? Am I trespassing, boss?" Laredo wiped blood from his face and spat back at Roarc.

"No, she is not! Pick up your gear and get out of here!"

Laredo slunk away muttering expletives. He headed for the bunk house and his things.

Mose heard the ruckus and returned. He stood watching anxiously. This could mean trouble because Laredo wasn't about to be bested in anything. Roarc had just made himself a bad enemy.

"Let's can these beans!" Mose's voice echoed around the yard. Mylena bent to gather the beans she had showered on Laredo. Roarc flexed his hand, then turned to face the scalding water bubbling in the large black pot. Soon they were all working diligently at their jobs of washing, blanching and filling jars with the garden's bounty. Thankfully Rian was busy in the barn with Olga and her pups so he was well out of their way.

They were always uneasy to have him playing around a pot of scalding water.

By mid-afternoon the jars were cooling on the back porch while Mose and Roarc cleared the yard of their work stations. Mylena bustled about the kitchen area with tired thoughts of what she would concoct for supper. Surely it wouldn't be green beans!

As Roarc read Rian a Bible story preparatory to his going up to bed, Mylena sat writing a letter to Julia, her friend back in Ohio. There was much to tell her. Their days here at the ranch were always busy with much to be accomplished.

"Hey, boss! It's Princess! I think her time has come?" Clint's voice shattered the quiet as Mylena lifted her pen once more. Roarc stopped in mid-sentence as Rian raised a sleepy head from against his father's chest.

"What?" Roarc set the little boy down and rose with alacrity at this summons. Princess was due to foal at any time—but this was a bit early to his way of thinking. He hoped nothing was wrong! He had a tidy sum tied up in this foal—aside from his fondness for the horse herself.

"I'll be right there!" He moved with lightening speed and crammed his hat on his head as he slammed out the back door.

"Why do men always have to wear their hats even in the dark?" Mylena muttered to no one in particular as she, too, laid down her pen and rose. Rian began to cry. He was alarmed at the hullabaloo and sleepy besides.

"Come on, honey. Let's get you up to bed." With her soothing words, he obeyed as they climbed the loft ladder. Soon he was stretched out on his feather bed but still sniffling.

"How about if I tell you a story?" Mylena stretched out beside him.

"What about?" His sniffling ceased immediately. "Do you know some stories?"

"Sure I do. My Mama used to tell me stories about a mother cat and her kittens when I was just about your size."

"Well—okay . . . . " Rian settled down to listen.

Before the story was half over he was asleep. Mylena smiled to herself remembering how she used to fall asleep just that same way before the story was finished. She closed her eyes for a moment to rest. It had been an extra long day canning green beans.

Roarc raced to Princess' stall to find her down and agitated. Clint held a lantern nearby as Roarc made a quick evaluation of the situation.

"Quick! Wake Mose and send Sam to get Grady at his house. Grady knows more about horses than anyone in this whole area. If there's a problem, he'll know what to do. Hurry!"

Soon Mose was kneeling beside Roarc at the mare's side. Roarc rubbed her head and uttered soothing words to calm her agitation. It looked like a long night ahead.

Mylena awoke with a start. Where was she? It was dark and the room smelled of hay.

Turning her head, she spied Rian sleeping soundly beside her. Then she knew exactly where she was.

She had been sleeping in Roarc's bed! But—where was he? Had he returned from the barn and found her there? Oh, she hoped not! Had he been forced to sleep downstairs?

She rose silently and made her way down the loft ladder. The lamp still burned low on the kitchen table where she had left it but the clock ticking above the mantle announced the time to be two o'clock in the morning. She tiptoed to peek into her bedroom. Was Roarc there? No, the bed was made just as she had left it this morning. Where was everyone? They must still be in the barn with Princess. She peered out the back door to find the barn alight with lanterns.

They probably all needed coffee by now. She hurried about the kitchen area making a big pot. When it was ready, she pulled a shawl about her shoulders and carried the hot pot carefully across the back yard to the barn. There she set it inside the work room and eased along to the men gathered outside Princess' stall.

Mose spied her first. "Why Miss Mylena, what are you doin' here?" All the men turned to stare at her. Confused, she gestured to the work room.

"I thought you might need some hot coffee so I brought a pot from the house . . . . "

"Well done, little lady!" Mose was the first to turn toward the work room where tin cups hung on nails along the wall waiting. He had soon poured cups of the hot brew for all the men gathering there. Roarc was the last to come in.

"Grady is with her. Thanks, Mylena, this hot coffee hits the spot. We have no idea how much longer it will be." He rubbed a hand across the back of his neck in a tired gesture.

Mylena smiled at the men as she turned to go back to the house. This was no place for her just now. "I'll see you in the morning then. Don't forget to bring the coffee pot back." She disappeared in the gloom of the wee hours.

A little before daylight Princess foaled with some help from Grady. There was a cheer in the barn at this success. The colt was a male with markings very similar to Roarc's stallion Arrow.

Roarc was extremely pleased. Grady offered to stay until breakfast so Roarc could get some rest.

Roarc stepped up on the back porch to find the lamp burning very low on the table and Mylena curled up asleep in his rocking chair. Had she stayed up all night? He was impressed. Lavina certainly would not have done that.

He stood over her for a moment, then stooped down and lifted her in his arms. She seemed sweet and sleepy and light as thistledown. He strode briskly to her bedroom, kicked open the door and deposited her across her bed. She turned to her side and sighed but never opened her eyes.

She must have been really tired after such a long day, he mused as he smiled, then turned to the loft ladder and his own bed

Rian awoke to find is father snoring deeply beside him in the dim loft light. It was morning and he suddenly remembered that Princess was supposed to have her baby today. He scooted around his sleeping father then made his way down the ladder. He peeked in Mylena's room as she was not in the kitchen and the big old stove was cold. What was going on?

He spied Mylena sound asleep across her bed still wearing her dress from yesterday. He was hungry and confused. He'd go find Mose.

Mose was making breakfast in the bunk house. "Well, howdy, boy, what are you doing out and about so early?"

"I just woke up—where is everybody? Papa and Miss Mylena are both asleep and I'm hungry."

"You just come on in and eat with us, boy. Then we'll show you Princess's new baby."

"It came?" Rian was all eyes at the thought.

"Sure it came. It's a male and pretty as can be."

It was a merry meal as the cow hands discussed the new arrival while Rian shoveled scrambled eggs into his mouth with gusto. Soon he was jumping down in a hurry to see the new foal.

Once in the barn, he headed for the stall where the new mama and her baby were. The mare snuffled her little one as he stood on wobbly legs and made small strides around the stall.

Rian was delighted.

"What will we name him?" His shrill little voice alerted the small animal causing it to raise its head in surprise.

Grady came to lean on the wooden planks forming the stall. "Well now, your Pa will have to name him. He will have an official name a mile long—but I'm sure you'll find a short nick-name for him."

The colt came forward and snuffled Rian's hand as he tried to touch the small animal's nose. Rian laughed with glee.

"I see you've met this new colt, son," As he came in, Roarc's voice interrupted Rian's giggles. He ruffled the boy's hair in a gesture of affection.

"Papa, he's perfect. What will we call him?"

"Let's give him a day or two to see what he does—then we'll think of a name for him."

Satisfied, Rian spent the morning in the barn romping with the half-grown pups and running back and forth to check on the new colt.

"We've gotta get rid of some of them dogs!" Mose grumbled as he wove his way through the throng of barkers to feed Princess her morning oats.

CHAPTER 7

Saturday dawned signaling a hot humid day. Mylena was up and about early in order to have her cooking done before the heat became too intense. Roarc and Rian had breakfasted in the bunk house where talk of the new colt was the main topic of conversation. This gave Mylena more time to bake a cake and insert a beef roast in the cavernous oven.

Roarc came to the back door with a message. "Grady said he and his boys might come today to pick up some of the pups. Do we have enough to invite them to eat with us?"

"Of course. Why don't you put one of the bunk house tables beneath that big old cottonwood tree and you and the boys can have your meal out there?

"Good idea." He moved off to do just that.

Before the hour was over, Mylena could hear Rian calling "Hello!" in his shrill little voice. She moved to peer out the front window. A wagon, filled with little boys, Grady driving the wagon and his wife seated beside him, was just pulling to a stop. Company! How nice!

Mylena whipped off her soiled apron towel, smoothed the curls of hair above her ears, and stepped to the front porch.

Little boys were everywhere along with barking pups. Rian was squealing with delight.

Grady helped his wife down from the wagon and Mylena could see that she was expecting once more.

Roarc came to greet them making introductions all around.

"This is Grady that you know and his wife, Vera. Welcome. This is Mrs. Mylena Harris who keeps house for us."

"It is so nice to meet another female," Mylena laughed. "Living around all these men can be a bit daunting now and then."

The men adjourned to the barn to inspect Princess and her foal while the little boys ran in all directions with the pups.

Mylena escorted Vera Grady into the house and seated her at the table. Soon they were both sipping from china cups rescued from the hutch.

"Tea—I haven't had tea in such a long time." Vera smiled. Her blonde hair was pulled atop her head and she fanned with her bonnet as she sipped.

"I know. It's a ladie's drink, isn't it? We used to have it back in Ohio but somehow it just doesn't seem right out here in Colorado among all these men."

In the wink of an eye the two became fast friends. They discussed sewing, new recipes, the latest trend in hats and then the due date for Vera's baby.

"It is supposed to be in October. I hope it will all be over before the holidays. That is such a busy time. I'm hoping for a girl. We lost our little girl two years ago so . . . . " her voice trailed off as tears filled her eyes.

Mylena was instantly contrite soothing Vera with comforting words.

"Mama! Mama!" The clatter of little boys perforated the peace of the house. "Sam wants my dog! Tell him to pick his own!"

Vera lumbered to the back door to referee their argument. They continued to disagree despite her words. Finally Mylena stepped to the door.

"These are still our dogs. If you boys can't agree, perhaps you don't need a dog at all."

Her firm words stopped the disagreement immediately. Not get a dog?

"But I wanted the tan one and Rian says I can't have him. He says he's keeping him."

Joe whined in discontent.

"That's exactly right. Now, let's see what the problem is." Mylena sat down on the porch steps as the boys gathered around. "Sam aren't you the oldest? Which dog did you like?"

"I wanted a spotted one but Jim . . . . "

"Then pick out the one you want. Jim will choose another one."

Sam moved to pick up a fat spotted pup that clearly resembled Olga.

"Fine. Now, Joe, you are next. How about the black one. That way you would never get them mixed up."

Joe eyed the black pup panting at his feet. After a moment he raised a smiling face.

"That's a good idea! I'll take him and call him Midnight." He grabbed the waiting pup and seemed quite pleased.

"What about me?" whined the littlest Jim. He was the youngest and he always seemed to get his way. Hmm, spoiled a bit, Mylena thought to herself.

"Well—you have the very best choice of all. Do you want a spotted pup to sometimes get mixed up with Sams—or do you want the white pup to be your very own Snowflake?"

A pleased smile broke across the youngster's face as he eyed the white pup laying in the shade nearby. He went over, patted the pup and was rewarded with a friendly lick from the pup's tongue. He giggled in delight and rolled on the grass beside the dog.

"Is that the one you want?" Mylena stood. The little boy nodded his head and put his arms about the white dog. Mylena shared a smile with Vera.

"I think we have that settled now, don't you?"

Once back inside, Vera whispered, "I don't know how you did that but it was exactly right. Were you a school teacher back in Ohio?"

"Oh, mercy no! I was simply a farmer's wife. I just remembered how my father used to settle things between me and my brother. We were so close in age, we were sometimes competitors in everything we did,"

The day was a howling success. Men, boys and dogs enjoyed their meal beneath the old cottonwood tree in the front yard. Vera and Mylena enjoyed a quieter time together inside visiting. By mid-afternoon Grady declared it was time to depart for home. Roarc and Mylena stood on the sparse lawn at the front of the house to wave them off. Their wagon disappeared amid a cloud of dust and barking pups.

Walt and China rode pell-mell into the ranch yard calling for Roarc.

"Hey, Boss, we've got trouble!"

Roarc was immediately alert. "What is it?"

"Someone cut our east fence and about twenty or thirty cows have escaped from our pasture. We'd better get that fence fixed quick before we lose more of them!"

"Were they rustled or did they just get out?"

"We could see some of them wandering off in the field next door—but not all of 'em of course. We really need to get that fence repaired and quick."

"Let's go on the double, boys." Roarc headed for the barn and his horse. Soon the crew of ranch hands had gathered, received their instructions and were riding off in several directions.

Mose came out to stand beside Mylena. He rubbed his chin and shook his grizzled head.

"Bet my boots Laredo is behind this . . . . "

By dark the fence had been repaired and some of the cattle returned to Roarc's pasture.

Two ranch hands volunteered to spend the night camping near the area to watch for the culprit, or culprits, who had cut the fence.

"They probably won't return to that area. They'll pick another site to destroy next."

Roarc was tired and dispirited as he rode in with his men.

Mylena had supper warming for him on the back of the stove. He washed up and sat down with a tired sigh.

"Was it bad?" Mylena poured herself a cup of coffee then sat at the table across from him.

"It could have been worse. We fixed the fence and the boys rounded up some of the cattle. But it makes me wonder who dislikes me enough to do that kind of damage."

"Mose suspects Laredo."

"So do I."

Mylena was quiet for a time, then she looked at Roarc with determination.

"I need to talk to you about something."

Roarc's heart sank again. Her visit with Vera Grady had probably stirred her up to want to leave. He dreaded to hear her next words. He swallowed the lump forming in his throat.

"All right."

"Visiting with the Gradys has made me realize we need to be in church. Those boys—and Rian—really do. Do you think it would be possible to go tomorrow?"

Surprised at this, Roarc was a bit slow in responding. That was not what he had been expecting to hear. He thought for a moment, then answered slowly.

"Well, I can't go tomorrow but maybe Mose can hitch up the buggy and take you and Rian in. The boys and I have more work to do in rounding up our missing cows."

"Oh, thank you! We'll be ready early."

Up before sunrise, Mylena made oatmeal for Rian and herself once more. A dollop of peach jam perked up the dish for Rian as she rushed him to eat and dress in his Sunday clothes.

"But what is church? Why can't Papa go too?"

"Your Papa has to work rounding up his cows today. Mose is going in with us. Hurry now so we won't make Mose wait for us."

Mylena shook out a dress she hadn't worn before. She had made herself a whole new wardrobe before leaving Ohio for she was not sure she would have access to a sewing machine for a long while. They had left almost everything behind with the house sale.

Now she twisted and turned before her mirror. It was still a good fit. With it she added a blue jacket and the little blue hat that traveled so well. Mose was waiting in the buggy so they were soon off to town.

It was a merry ride as Mose was full of tales about his early days as a cowboy.

"One time when I was riding trail to Montana me and my buddy spied a bear cub just about half-grown. Wild as we were then, we decided to try roping him. Well we twirled our ropes and spun them out. I missed. But my buddy's lasso ringed that bear cub's neck. We whooped with glee.

But that bear cub was nobody's fool. He turned and started climbing that rope right up to that horse's neck." He laughed loud and long.

"What happened then?" Rian's eyes were big as saucers.

"When that bear cub hit that horse, my buddy got thrown. He went flying through the air like a balloon."

"Was he hurt?"

"We thought he was but he turned out to be all right. We just had a bad time trying to catch his horse after that."

Rian never tired of hearing him talk. Before they knew it, they were entering the town.

"Where shall I stop, Miss Mylena?"

"Take us to the church. We'll get out and then we'll meet you after the service in the church yard. Will that be fine with you?"

Mose nodded his agreement as he reined in the horses. Several buggies and wagons were parked near the little white little church. People were going in as Mylena and Rian followed.

They moved along the aisle until Mylena spotted Louise Wilson sitting well toward the front of the building. She scooted in beside her leaving Rian on the end of the pew. He looked around in wide-eyed wonder until he spotted a small girl with long yellow curls smiling at him. He settled down with a bashful grin.

Mylena was able to explain to Louise why they were here today. Louise was delighted as she clasped Mylena's hand lovingly.

"You must have dinner with the doctor and me at the hotel dining room then," she whispered just as the song leader rose to announce the first number in the hymnal.

Across the aisle sat Roland Hamilton, his stick-thin wife Martha, and his only son, Boyd. Roland Hamilton was the town banker, supposedly the richest man in town many whispered. Boyd had returned the past week from a six months seminar on banking in Boston. He had dreaded his return to "the sticks" as he called Callahan. Now he surveyed Mylena as she took her place across the aisle. He nudged his father.

"Who is that woman?"

Impervious as usual, Roland answered, "That's the two widows from the train massacre I told you about. The older one works for Dr. Sims and the other one works for Roarc Rhynhart. That's his little boy she takes care of."

Boyd Hamilton smoothed his pencil-thin mustache and crossed his well-shod feet. Hmm, perhaps life in "the sticks" wouldn't be so bad after all. Widows were well-known for needing attention after losing their man . . . . He heard very little of the service as he eyed Mylena's perfect profile.

Louise introduced Mylena and Rian to the minister as they left. A little man with no hair and gold-rimmed glasses, he offered an enthusiastic welcome. Boyd Hamilton made sure he was right behind the two as they shook the minister's hand. He stepped right up and introduced himself as well.

He seemed to hold Mylena's hand a bit longer than necessary she thought but perhaps he was just being polite. Maybe that was the eastern custom these days.

"It's been a while since I've seen two such lovely ladies in our little town," he seemed to gush. "We need to become better acquainted. Would you dine with me and my family in the hotel dining room?"

Louise made their reply. "Oh, I'm so sorry but we're to meet Dr. Sims there for dinner today. Perhaps some other Sunday would be fine."

"Yes, I'm sure. If I may be so bold, perhaps I might call on you one day." He acquiesced politely but he grimaced as they turned to walk down the street. He muttered to himself, "Not you, you old crow, the other one."

Two weeks passed quietly. Mylena was reluctant to ask for another trip to town to attend church so soon. The men were inordinately busy working cattle and preparing for harvest which would soon be upon them.

"Rian's birthday is coming up. I think it's time he had a horse of his own." Roarc spoke softly to Mose one evening in the quiet of the bunkhouse porch. "I want it to be a surprise. I've started looking around for just the right one so if anyone mentions this to you, you'll know why." Mose grinned and nodded his head in agreement.

Boyd Hamilton, disappointed that Mylena had not returned to church in two weeks, decided to call on her at the Rhynhart ranch. He chose a Sunday afternoon, hot and sultry, with puffs of white clouds roaming the blue sky. It was farther from town than he remembered but he trotted on.

Seeing the lovely widow once more would be worth the trip.

Mylena was seated on the front porch shelling crowder peas. Rian was lazing on the porch floor with his slate as Mylena taught him some new words and how only one letter could change the name of an animal . . . . c-a-t to r-a-t . . . . d-o-g to h-o-g . . . . c-o-w to s-o-w. He was fascinated as he wrote the letters on his slate.

A sudden cloud of dust heralded the arrival of a visitor. Then the clop of hooves on hard ground accented the arrival of a snappy black buggy. Black leather trimmed in red and hitched to a coal black horse, the vehicle looked brand-new.

Roarc was standing at the windmill drinking from the dipper hanging there. His eye caught the elegant contraption and the dapper young man stepping from it. Looked like a funeral vehicle to him, he mused as he strode to offer a friendly hand shake.

Mylena rose from her chair and set the bowl of crowder peas aside. Rian stood and stared. Who was this? It looked like that man they met at church. It was.

He came smiling up the porch steps introducing himself. "I'm Boyd Hamilton from Callahan. I'm in banking with my father there. I'm sure you remember him."

"Of course," Roarc offered a friendly welcome silently wondering what the man was doing here—and on a Sunday afternoon. But it was soon apparent as Hamilton took Mylena's hand and held it for an interminably long time.

"Good afternoon, Mrs. Harris. I trust you've been well. We haven't seen you in town lately. I've missed seeing your ravishing face."

How oily could the man be? Roarc suddenly realized the man had come to call on Mylena. His dander rose. He hooked a cane bottom chair with his boot and sat down to stay.

A bit flustered, Mylena could only blush at the man's flirtatious words. What would Roarc think? Probably that she had been flirting even at church!

Sensing her surprise, Roarc added to the confusion deliberately.

"Our Mylena makes a delicious lemonade. Would you care for some, Mr. Hamilton?"

"That would be very nice," Boyd agreed as he, too, sat in a cane bottom chair.

Mylena scurried away as Rian followed.

"Quick, Rian, hand me some lemons from the storage room. I hope there will be enough to make a decent lemonade. Now, run to the windmill and bring me a bucket of cold water. That's a good boy!" Rian obeyed without demur for he loved lemonade.

Soon Mylena returned with tall glasses of the delicious drink in glasses purloined from the hutch where Lavina's fancy dishes were still displayed. They came in handy when company came.

Perversely Roarc remained seated the entire time. Boyd Hamilton didn't have a moment alone with the pretty widow. At last he rose with a polite "good evening" and strode to his waiting buggy. With a wave of his hand, he turned the vehicle and trotted into the distance. He muttered to himself as he rode along.

"I'll just have to reach her when she's in town. That rancher has an eye on her himself.

What a wasted afternoon!"

CHAPTER 8

Later in the afternoon, after Roarc had left the porch, Mylena sat thinking of the events of the day. Roarc had seemed overtly polite to their visitor. He had thanked her nicely for the lemonade declaring it delicious as he swung down from the porch. A cloud of dust rose as the black buggy disappeared in the distance. He had made no remark about her possible flirting while in town. She was thankful for this. She certainly had not encouraged Boyd Hamilton in any way. She stopped her thoughts in shock. Why should she care what Roarc thought? Why indeed? But she did. Desperately.

A sudden shout seemed to come from the corrals. All eyes turned to spy Walt and Sim riding in pell-mell with dust flying from their horse's hooves. They dismounted in a hurry to face Roarc and Mose already waiting at the corral gate.

"We've got more trouble, Roarc! The south windmill has been shot all to pieces. The water tank is full of holes and empty. Cattle are bawling for water out there."

This brought on a hurried consultation for all. Roarc himself saddled Arrow and rode out with the two to inspect the situation. Those left behind began to gather up supplies. They would be out early the next morning with repairs.

Mylena guided Rian back into the house to prepare their evening meal.

"Why is someone always trying to hurt us?" Rian whined.

"I think someone is mad at your Papa. He thinks it may be Laredo because he fired him. I don't know. Your Papa heard he's working at the Chidister place now—and that's not very far from here."

Grady came to help with he windmill repairs. He had information Roarc had suspected for some time. Quietly he confided his news to Roarc.

"I'm just sure I saw three or four of your cows over at the Chidister place last week. I was over there checking out one of the horses that had run through a barb-wire fence. The brands on the cows had been changed a little bit—but I recognized 'em just the same. What you gonna do about that?"

Roarc rubbed his chin in thought. "I'm not sure. I hate to accuse Chidister and make an enemy of him—but I still think Laredo is our culprit. All I can do right now is watch and wait until he does something I can pin on him—and he will."

Rian's birthday arrived in the form of a hot, sultry day. They were beginning to really need rain. Their crops were wilting in the fields and the cattle were needing deeper grass. Roarc and Mose had a secret. Not even Mylena had been trusted with it.

The day before Roarc had asked her if she and Rian would take some food to Mrs. Grady as she wasn't feeling too well. China would take them in the buggy as he and Mose had some chores they needed to finish.

Perplexed, Mylena agreed. She stirred up a butter cake and made a peach cobbler to take the Grady family. Early on Rian's birthday, China brought the buggy around and Clint seemed to be riding shot-gun beside them.

"Why is Clint riding beside us?" she asked Roarc quietly as he set the cobbler safely inside the buggy floor.

"Because I don't want you and Rian to encounter any trouble along the way. We never know who is doing the damage to our ranch. I just want you two to be safe." His determined stare into her own blue eyes allayed her fears.

The ride to the Grady place was uneventful. Boys and dogs met them with a clatter of noise. Vera Grady hobbled to the door, round and heavy with child.

"Why, Miss Mylena, how nice to see you!" She was very grateful for the food and couldn't thank Mylena enough.

"It was really Roarc's idea. I didn't know you weren't feeling well. I could have been here long before now."

They did not stay for dinner. The food was for the Grady family. Trotting home, Mylena felt a glow of happiness at having been of help to someone as needy as Vera Grady. She really had her hands full.

Rian chattered all the way. "I told them it was my birthday and they wanted to know what my Papa gave me. I told them nothing and they laughed. They said it wasn't really my birthday—that I was just making that up." His downcast face melted Mylena's heart.

As China guided the buggy home, he took them directly to the barn. Mylena wondered why but she didn't have time to argue. Roarc and Mose came out with wide grins on their faces. All the ranch hands gathered around as Rian and Mylena stepped down from the buggy.

Roarc turned, opened wide the barn door and led out a small paint pony. It shook its head and snuffled his hand as Rian's eyes grew round in his pale face.

"Happy Birthday, son," Roarc presented the reins to the boy.

"Is he mine?" Rian was ecstatic. He inspected the small saddle and walked around and around the horse. He patted his flanks timidly. Then he rubbed the pony's neck.

"Here, give him this apple." Mose handed the boy the treat.

The pony snuffled Rian, then took the apple pieces in his mouth greedily. Chewing lustily he snuffled Rian again amid the boy's giggles. "He's really mine?"

"Sure enough," Roarc grinned at his son's pleasure. The entire group clapped their hands and wished the boy a happy birthday. Now Mylena understood why they had been banished to the Grady's today. Roarc had to have the paint pony delivered secretly while Rian was away.

"This is the best birthday ever!" Rian declared as he carefully mounted the small animal and rode round the corral.

Roarc turned and placed an arm about Mylena's shoulder. He whispered, "I think he likes him, don't you?"

Mylena was shocked at the electric tingle that sizzled all the way to her toes at Roarc's touch. He had never done such a thing before. She could only stand very still as the sizzle subsided into a warm glow of affection. Was she falling for the hard-headed rancher?

Then he was gone calling to Rian something Mylena did not listen to. She turned to make her way slowly to the house. She had never felt this way with Will. She was afraid. She couldn't afford to love Roarc Rhynhart. He didn't want a woman in his life. He had already made that very clear.

Saturday rolled around once more—and it was shopping day. Roarc drove the wagon with Mylena beside him while Mose and Rian rode behind. They needed everything to her way of thinking. They were getting low on flour and sugar and she hoped to find some canned fruit in Mr. Dickens store.

But once in town, things were hopping. They all went their separate ways taking care of their own needs. Rian ran up to Mylena as she entered Mr. Dicken's store.

"There's a street dance tonight. There's a bar-b-que supper and then the dance. Can we stay, Miss Mylena? Can we?"

"Well I don't know, Rian. You'll have to ask your Papa."

"Oh, he'll stay if YOU want to. I'll go find him." He was off quicker than lightening.

"Rian, wait . . . . " but she was too late. He had already disappeared. She put a hand to her mouth in consternation. She hoped Roarc would not think SHE had suggested this!

But later, as she was paying for her few purchases, Mose came into the store.

"Roarc says we'll stay if you want to, Mylena. Things are beginning to start early now."

It was true. People were gathering beneath the trees at the end of town where huge pits were filled with the aroma of roasting meat. Makeshift tables had been set up and some of the ladies were serving food to a line of hungry visitors.

Mose escorted Mylena into the line of waiting diners. Before long a breathless Rian ran up to join them. Then Roarc left his friends and added his long, lean body to their wait as hunger pangs seemed to dominate the evening.

At last it was their turn to chose a plate. Very carefully they carried them to an empty table and sat down to enjoy the feast. Several patrons were already drinking beer but Mose and Roarc did not join them. Roarc seemed to keep a watchful eye on everything and everyone.

As dusk settled over the scene, musicians came out and began tuning their instruments.

Mylena thought of how often she had seen Will do this. She did not think of Will very much—only occasionally and with brotherly fondness. Sometimes this worried her. If she had loved her husband as she should, wouldn't she grieve more for him?

Then Rian asked to be off with some of his friends and Roarc agreed with a stipulation that he stay nearby in the dim lights. "No running off into the dark, son. I want to be able to find you when we're ready to go home."

"Yes, sir!" and he was galloping off with his friends.

"Mose, I see Chidister over there. I think I'll go talk to him." Roarc gathered their empty plates and wove his way through the crowd.

"Why, Mrs. Harris, how nice to find you here." Boyd Hamilton sat down beside her.

"Ah-oh," thought Mose as he eyed the dapper visitor. His clothes were of the latest fashion and his pencil-thin mustache added a touch of elegance to his arrogant face.

When the music started, Boyd insisted they "take a turn across the floor." Mylena really had no excuse so she agreed a bit reluctantly. Soon he was swinging her in the latest steps amid the throng of dancers. He somehow seemed to monopolize her all evening. His silver tongue turned away all comers until a tall, seedy cowboy loomed beside them.

Mylena turned. It was Laredo!

"I see you're having a good time, Miss Mylena. This next dance is mine." He glared at Boyd Hamilton with a steely-eyed determination. There seemed to be an evil dare in his dark eyes.

But before he could swing her away, Roarc intervened.

"No, you're wrong, Laredo. This dance is MINE." Roarc was bigger, stronger and more deft on his feet. He whirled Mylena away before either man could say a word.

Mylena had danced with Roarc once before. His hard arms held her tenderly as he swung her about. He looked down into her face and smiled.

"I think it's about time we headed for home, don't you?"

"Yes," she whispered as he swung her once more near the edge of the dance floor.

As the music stopped, he led her down the steps and through the crowd to the wagon where Mose was waiting with a tired but happy Rian sitting in the back among their purchases.

The long ride home in the soft moonlight was a halcyon time for Mylena. Mose drove the horses while Roarc sat with an arm about her to steady her in the seat. At least that's what she told herself as she rode along. His thigh nudged hers as the scent that was his alone wafted about her.

Back home Mose stopped the wagon. Roarc swung Mylena down and smiled a soft "good night". Then he lifted a sleepy Rian from the wagon bed and set him on his feet at her side The pair went to the house as the men took the wagon to the barn to stable it overnight.

Mose walked back toward the bunkhouse with Roarc.

"You gonna let that little gal get away? She was mighty popular tonight."

"Now, Mose, you know I'm not in the market for a bride." Roarc slapped Mose on the shoulder and, laughing, strode on toward the house

Mose stood in the moonlight with a disgusted look on his face.

"Mule-headed, contrary critter. He can't see the forest for the trees!"

Laredo was incensed as he watched Roarc lead Mylena from the dance floor only to disappear in the crowd. His anger and hate for Roarc surged within him. He clenched his fists. He vowed to do even more damage to that hated enemy!

Boyd Hamilton was a bit bewildered at this turn of events. They had certainly disappeared in a hurry. He would almost swear that rancher had his own eye on the pretty little widow. Well—time would tell. He smoothed his mustache as he made his way through the crowd.

It was time to harvest the corn and all hands were in the fields except Mylena. She was cooking for the crew and it took all her time. Even Rian was out there learning the rhythm of corn harvesting. True he didn't get a lot done but he was still trying—hard.

As she stirred a large pan of cornbread batter, she heard the clatter of hooves coming from the lane beside the barn. It must be someone coming from Grady's. She peered out the window to find Joe Grady riding their old gray horse bareback. He jumped down and came running to the back door.

"Miss Mylena, come quick. Pa and Ma need you. Ma's taken real bad."

"Oh, Joe, of course I'll come! Run to the corn patch and tell Roarc that I need to go."

She bustled about turning off the stove and setting the batter aside. She snatched off her apron towel and ran her hands across her hair. Could she go like this?

Suddenly Roarc was at the back door. Joe was leaping astride the old gray horse and heading for home once more.

"Mylena? Ready to go?"

"Yes! Yes I am! Let's go! But where is the buggy?"

"All the horses are being used harvesting the corn—all except Arrow. Come on, we can ride him double as far as Gradys."

He lifted her atop the saddle and swung on behind, then, with a tug of the reins and a kick to Arrow's middle, they were off at a gallop. Roarc held Mylena tightly as they moved across the hard ground.

Finally she squirmed in his hold to almost yell. "Stop and let me ride astride. We'd make better time."

"Are you sure? In that dress?"

"Yes, I'm sure! I've done it many times before with my brother in Ohio."

Roarc slowed the horse as Mylena swung one leg across the saddle to sit astride.

Roarc grasped her about the waist and they galloped on until the Grady house loomed in the distance.

Grady's little boys, Sam and Jim, were fighting and yelling in the yard. They were swinging pieces of wood at each other in abandon. Roarc stopped the horse and helped Mylena down. In spite of her trying to keep her distance, she slid all the way down Roarc's body until she reached the ground. Looking up, she noted a very strange expression on his handsome face. But she didn't have time to think about that now—Vera Grady needed her. She ran swiftly into the house.

Roarc roared at the two fighting boys.

"You two toss that wood under the boiling pot and stop that fighting. Then you both get busy rounding up more wood for the fire. Hop to it, now, before I call your Pa to straighten you out."

They instantly obeyed his commanding voice.

Joe came across the yard leaving the horse panting by the barn.

"Joe, don't you know how to brush down a horse after a hard ride?"

"Yes sir."

"Well—go do it. That horse needs attention now that you're back."

Again obedience was the order of the day as Joe swung away to care for the waiting animal. Roarc entered the house to meet Grady coming out.

"She's bad, Roarc. I'm scared. It isn't time for the babe to come. If she loses this one I don't know what we'll do." He rubbed a tired hand across his face.

"We're here to help, Grady. Just tell us what to do."

Mylena found Vera writhing on the bed amid soft moans. She knelt beside the bed and took Vera's hand in hers.

"Oh, Mylena, I'm so glad you're here. I'm so scared for the baby. It's too early!"

"Maybe this little one is just ready to come out and see the light of day. We'll do our best to help it in any way we can."

Soothed by Mylena's words, Vera settled down to take tiny naps between contractions.

Roarc finally settled the boys down with a game of marbles. He played with them amid much hilarity but he kept one eye on the door to the house in case he was needed.

A shrill cry filled the air. It was a baby's cry, tiny and fragile.

Jim looked up. "Is Ma having another baby?"

Sam said, "Aw gee, we don't need another baby."

Joe added, "Na, we got enough."

Roarc shushed them with a hard look. "Do you mean you boys don't have room in your hearts for another little brother or sister? Shame on you. What if that was said when YOU were being born? How would you feel then?"

The trio of boys sobered and seemed to be seriously thinking about this.

Grady came out to stand on the porch. His tired demeanor was evident.

"It's a girl. But it's premature. I don't know if she will live or not."

Roarc stepped through the door to find Mylena wrapping the tiny baby in a warm blanket, placing it beside Vera and adding a hot water bottle to its side.

"Can I do anything?"

"Not right now. Be sure to keep lots of hot water going as we will need to keep this hot water bottle warm all the time. I saw this happen once back in Ohio. We saved the baby with just such attention night and day. We'll try our best to do it here."

Later, as Grady visited with Vera while they showed the wee new baby to the boys, Roarc led Mylena to the porch.

"Will you stay a few days?"

"Yes, of course I will. But I will need some clean clothes."

"I'll bring them first thing in the morning."

"But—you won't know what to bring . . . . "

"Remember now—I've been married. I know what ladies wear." Roarc's chuckle rang out softly in the quiet evening air.

Mylena felt herself blushing as she smiled as well.

It was a week before she was able to return to the ranch. By that time, Grady had persuaded Grandma Kelly to come stay with them until Vera was well again. Grandma Kelly made her living staying with new mothers and babies all over the area.

Vera's baby seemed to be thriving with such good care. Mylena felt she was able to return home at last. Roarc had ridden by every night to check on them. Mylena had begun to look forward to his visits more and more each day. They often sat on the porch to recount their day as Grady put the boys to bed.

"Tomorrow I'm taking you home," Roarc announced as they stood in the moonlight one late August evening.

"Will you bring the buggy?"

"Nope. I'm coming on Arrow just like I brought you here."

"But I have clothes to take back this time . . . . "

"We'll tie them in a bundle and hang them on Arrow's saddle. He's big enough to carry everything."

True to his word, Roarc arrived after supper the next night. Mylena was ready and, after a tearful farewell with Vera and her new little girl, Mylena allowed Roarc to lift her atop the saddle. His strong hands about her waist sent a frisson of feeling to her toes. He swung up behind her, put his arms about her and reined Arrow toward home.

Nestled in Roarc's arms, Mylena thoroughly enjoyed the ride in the moonlight. Roarc was full of news of the happenings at the ranch that week. Mylena found herself laughing at the antics he recounted of Rian and Paint Pony. The ride wasn't nearly long enough to her way of thinking. He rode almost to the back door of the ranch house before he stopped. Swinging down from the saddle, he lifted Mylena from the horse's back. She slid slowly down, down his body until her feet finally touched the ground. Roarc kept his hard arms about her for long moments. With one hand he tilted his hat to the back of his head and lowered his lips to hers in the lightest of kisses.

"Goodnight, lady. I'm glad you're home," he whispered as he reluctantly released her.

Stunned, Mylena stood for a moment, then turned and fled into the dark recess of the house. She didn't stop until she reached her room. She slammed the door and sat on the bed breathless.

Roarc had kissed her! She put her fingers to her lips in amazement. She still felt the flutter in her mid-section the touch of his lips had caused. She was overwhelmed with feeling—feeling she had never experienced before. True, she had been kissed before—but never with the electric effect Roarc's mouth had elicited. She sat for long moments. She finally had to admit it. She was falling fathoms in love with the handsome rancher. But—where would it lead? He seemed perfectly content to be single.

Sadly she rose, slipped off her clothing and donned the nightgown hanging behind the door. He had missed bringing it to her at Gradys—he had found a clean one in her dresser drawer. The thought of him going through her intimate apparel sent a strange shiver through her. She brushed out her hair in the moonlight beaming through her window, then lay down. Tired from her days work at Gradys, she was soon fast asleep.

Roarc stabled Arrow, then made his way to the house. Rian had been spending nights with Mose in the bunkhouse since Mylena had been gone so the boy was not sleeping in the loft tonight. Roarc set the bundle of Mylena's clothing in her rocking chair, then climbed the loft ladder to undress and lay thinking, alone. Arms behind his dark head, he felt again the shape of Mylena's body against his as they rode through the moonlight. He tasted in memory the sweetness of her lips as he remembered their shared kiss. It had been so long . . . . too long . . . .

It felt good to know she was again downstairs in her own bed. The house had been dreadfully lonely while she was gone to Gradys. He had missed her cheery smile—her lithe way of moving about the house—the pleasant aroma of her cooking . . . .

What would it be like to have her here all the time—permanently?

CHAPTER 9

Roarc and his cowboys were still puzzled as to where the missing cows could be. The boys had ridden all over their pasture in every direction checking on things, searching for some clue as to where the vagrant animals could be. At last they had to admit someone had stolen then.

Reluctantly Roarc decided to pay Cal Chidister a visit He certainly didn't want to accuse the neighbor—but something had to be done.

"Clint, you and China come with me. China can spot a brand that has been tampered with quicker than anyone I know. Let's saddle up and ride."

Chidister's ranch was not so large nor so orderly as Roarc's. Chidister was definitely middle-aged and tired of hard work. He left most of the day-to-day chores to his foreman, Jose. He came out on his front porch as the three riders came into view.

"Looks like company comin'."

Greetings were exchanged all around as he invited them in for coffee. Roarc doffed his Stetson and declined politely.

"No thanks, Cal. We're on a working trip today. We're looking for some cows that have wandered off our land. We can't find them anywhere so we wondered if you would mind our looking in your south pasture to see if any of them wandered over there. Our fence was cut a while back so you know how those critters like to roam."

"Sure I do. You go on over and look around. Jose keeps tabs on my herd so he might know."

"Good. If you don't mind, we'll check in with him." With a nod and a wave, the three reined their mounts and rode off south.

Laredo was watching from the shade of the barn. With a mouthful of expletives, he turned to his buddy, Satch, forking hay nearby.

"You got them cows stashed away good?"

"Sure have."

"You'd better!" Laredo threw down his cigarette and stomped off.

"Hey, you better stamp that cig out! What if you catch this hay on fire? We'd get fired for sure!" Satch bellowed at Laredo's retreating back. He never looked around.

Half a day's ride disclosed what Roarc had feared. In a small pasture bounded by new barb-wire, they found two dozen of their cows.

"See them brands? They've been burned over with another curlicue changing the shape of your brand. The scabs are still seeping so they aren't very old." China was quick to point out their find.

Other breeds of cattle were present so they took a look at them as well. Sure enough they also bore evidence of old brands being tampered with.

"These look like someone was playing with Chidister's cows too. That's his brand under the new one." China was positive of his find.

"Well I'll be . . . . " Roarc and Clint exchanged shocked looks.

"Looks like someone here on Chidister's ranch is stealing his cattle too. He needs to know about this."

Dust flew behind their horses as the three rode back to find Cal Chidister sitting on his porch puffing a cigar. He welcomed them once more with a wide grin.

"Howdy, boys, any news?"

"I'd say so, sir. You won't believe what we've found."

Chidister had to ride out himself, along with Jose, to see what the men had found. He was angry. At first he blamed Jose; then he realized Jose had been with him for twenty years. It couldn't have been him or cattle would have disappeared long ago.

"Why them so and sos! I'll bet it's the two new men I hired last month! Already stealing from me!" Expletives flew once more. "You'd better ride in to town and get the sheriff. I want him to know about this."

"Yes, if they can steal a couple of dozen from me, then twenty or so from you, and probably raid another ranch around here like that,—it wouldn't be long before they had enough cows to fill a boxcar of their own. Then they could ride all the way to Kansas City and collect a tidy sum for themselves. Quite a racket!"

"They had them all stashed away in this far pasture—and even had strung a new fence to keep them in. Those sorry rats!" Cal Chidister was inconsolable in his anger.

Sheriff Gilless rode back with Clint from town. He took a look around and decided the culprits were probably Chidister's new hands all right. He agreed to put out a warrant for their arrest. Jose rounded up his boss's cows while Roarc and his men headed out with theirs.

Tomorrow brands would need to be changed back—as best they could—more work when they needed it the least.

September was upon them. The corn had been gathered and stored; the small cotton crop had been picked and the garden produce had either been sold or canned. The days had been busy for them all. Now it was time to ship their cattle to market. Fat from the long summer grass, the cow hands herded them into the corrals preparatory to taking them to the railroad for shipping to Kansas City.

Roarc came into the kitchen area where Mylena was drying her last dish. She stored it safely away in the cabinet and turned questioning eyes to his serious face.

"What is it?"

Roarc slapped his gloves against his thigh and eyed her. He didn't know if she would listen to him or not—but he needed to try to make her understand the situation.

"We're taking the cattle to the railroad starting tomorrow early. Clint, Walt and Sim will go along with me. China will stay here with Mose. I want you and Rian to go to the Gradys for about three days while we're away with the herd."

"Go to the Gradys? Why? They are doing fine with Grandma Kelly there."

"No, now listen to me. It's for your safety and Rians. Remember he is MY son after all and I want him safe. With Laredo still in the picture, we run the risk of his deciding to come here when he realizes most of us are gone. I don't want you here alone."

"But you said Mose and China would be here . . . . "

"Mylena, please don't argue with me about this. Laredo has been arrested twice since he has been in Callahan for molesting women in the saloons. I didn't know this when I hired him. He is one of the best cowboys around—but his reputation with women is bad. Do you think Mose or China, with his crippled leg, would be a match for Laredo? I don't. I want you and Rian safe while I am away.

Do you understand?"

Reluctantly she nodded her head. He was, after all, Rian's father so she had to listen.

"Very well. When do we leave?" Her voice was cool but controlled.

"We take the herd about daylight tomorrow. China will take you and Rian to Gradys right after breakfast."

"Fine. We'll be ready." She turned away. She definitely did not relish obeying his orders—but he WAS the boss.

The cattle pens were five miles from town. Roarc had made arrangements to have his herd loaded from the cattle chutes there where his men herded the bawling animals into boxcars to carry then all the way to Kansas City. Clint and Walt would go along to finalize their sale at the cattle yards in the city. Then they would return by rail.

Roarc sold twenty-five head of his cows to a rancher from the north of the state who was needing to improve his stock. With the money safely in his pocket, he waved Clint and Walt off as they hung out of a boxcar from the slowly moving train. He smiled. Those two would have a rousing good time in Kansas City. He just hoped they wouldn't get drunk, get into a poker game and lose all his money from the sale. He grinned to himself. They were good men. He trusted them.

Riding back into Callahan, he decided to deposit the money from his sale to the northern rancher in the bank. He reined in, tied Arrow to a nearby hitching post, and strode into the bank's interior. His transaction concluded, he started for the door when he was hailed by Boyd Hamilton who came from around his desk with an officious smile.

"Mr. Rhynhart—Roarc—" Boyd shook Roarc's hand in his soft non-calloused fingers.

"Did they take care of you? Everything going well at the ranch?"

"Fine—and yes, they did. How are you, Hamilton?"

With a few more platitudes, Boyd got down to the business in hand. "I need to speak with you about something important. I have an interest in your housekeeper, Mrs. Harris. Is she spoken for with you?"

Surprised, Roarc found himself floundering for an answer.

"Not that I know of . . . . "

"In that case I need to inform you that I want to state my intention to court her with the possibility of asking her to marry me. It's time I settled down here in Callahan with a wife and family. She seems an ideal companion." His facetious smile sent a bolt of anger through Roarc.

"Well—you'll just have to ask her about that, won't you?" Roarc's short reply ended their conversation. He strode briskly out, mounted Arrow and reined him toward home.

Boyd Hamilton stood at the bank window staring at his abrupt departure. That should put a period to Rhynhart's continual surveillance when Boyd came around. Now maybe he would have a clear shot at courting the lady in question. But he still wondered . . . .

Laredo watched the dust of the herd of cattle as they made their way to the loading chutes. Hmmm. Old Roarc was sending his cattle off to market today. Hmmm. Bet Miss Mylena was home alone. Bet he'd better check that out.

He didn't follow the main road. He veered off and approached the ranch from the side. No smoke seemed to be coming from the chimney of the house. Odd. He could make out Mose and China working with a horse in the corral. No one else seemed to be about. Great!

He tied his horse to a small tree north of the house and crept to the front porch. It was dark inside so he could see very little. No fire glowed in the fireplace. He ducked around to the back door and eased it open. If Mylena was here, the coast was clear.

He tiptoed through the main room searching for her. He opened her bedroom door to find the room empty. He stealthily climbed the loft ladder until he could look all about the loft. Nothing there except a bed, a small table and an unlit lamp.

Disgusted, he moved out the back door and dodged through the back yard to peer into the chicken house. The squawk of chickens heralded his approach. He hunkered down behind the fence until the chickens settled down. Mylena wasn't there.

He dared not go any closer to the barn. Old Mose had eyes in the back of his head so he would spot him in a minute. After a concentrated survey of the outbuildings, he dodged back to his horse and headed back to town. Where could Mylena be?

Mylena was having the time of her life. Vera Grady had her sewing machine out and waiting. She laid several dresses on the bed beside where Mylena was depositing the carpet bag she had packed for her and Rian for their three day visit.

"I need these dresses to fit again. Can you take them up so they'll have a waist?"

Mylena shook the dresses out and turned them inside out.

"Oh yes. There is plenty of material here. I can re-cut them and stitch them to fit.

It will be fun!" She set about the task immediately.

Rian was already busy playing a game with the Grady boys. Mylena was glad there wasn't a tree with branches low enough for them to climb. She could relax a bit and get to her sewing.

Three days later Vera was the proud owner of not three, but four, dresses that fit. She was a petite blonde woman, very pretty. With the birth of her baby daughter, she seemed to have come out of her shell and was a laughing, lovable woman once more.

Saturday found them again in town for shopping. Mylena sought out Louise Wilson as soon as she had finished selecting the items she needed. Louise was, as usual, busy in the doctor's office writing up medical records. Doctor Sims came out of his office with a wide smile on his face.

"Have you heard the news?"

"No, I haven't. What?" Mylena's answering smile invited his confidence.

"Louise, here, has agreed to be my bride. We've set the wedding for next Friday night. You will come, won't you?"

Louise rose from her chair to share a hug with Mylena. She blushed as Mylena stood back to see her reaction to the doctor's announcement. Then her smile belied her embarrassment.

"I know it's awfully soon but—well, it just didn't seem important to wait any longer."

She lifted her eyes to share a loving smile with the gray-haired man beside her.

"Why that's wonderful! Of course, I'll be here—just tell me the time and place!"

A happy hour was spent as the trio outlined plans for the upcoming nuptials.

Mylena glanced at the lapel watch she wore on her jacket. "It's time for me to go meet the men with the wagon. I'll be here on Friday. You can count on it." She made her goodbyes and rushed out the door. She was running late. They had been so engrossed in the plans for Friday she had lost track of time. She really had to hurry.

Suddenly someone loomed before her on the boardwalk. It was Boyd Hamilton.

"Mrs. Harris—or may I call you Mylena?" He doffed his hat and smiled facetiously.

Surprised, Mylena found herself stammering in her confusion.

"Well—yes—of course."

"I see you have been visiting with Dr. Sims and his future bride. I want to invite you to be my guest at the wedding and all the festivities following next Friday night. Please say yes."

Mylena regained her equilibrium as she replied.

"That would be very nice but I'm not sure how I'll be coming to town . . . ."

"Oh, that is no problem. I'll come for you in my buggy and I'll see you home after."

What could she do but agree? She had no previous plans to fall back on.

""Well—I suppose that would be fine." She offered a small smile and extended her hand as if to conclude an agreement.

Boyd took her hand in his and held it for long minutes. Then, with a fond farewell, he kissed her hand with a flourish and let her go.

All the way home Mylena chattered about the upcoming wedding. The men were thoroughly tired of hearing about it long before the ranch loomed in sight.

"How you gonna get to town on Friday?" asked Mose thoughtfully. Maybe Roarc would take the hint. He didn't.

"Oh, Mr. Hamilton is calling for me and will see me home after. I have it all arranged."

She shot a quick glance at Roarc's profile as he guided the team. His expression gave nothing away. He just didn't seem to be very sociable to her way of thinking.

The week passed slowly for Mylena as she looked forward to the wedding party. Even the thought of Boyd Hamilton escorting her seemed to recede into the background as she planned what she would wear and a present for the bride and groom.

Roarc seemed unusually grouchy all week. Mose grinned to himself. He bet he knew why. But he kept his own counsel. No need to rile Roarc up any more than usual.

Mylena was a little hurt by Roarc's indifference to her friend's wedding. But by the time Friday evening arrived, Mylena tossed her curls and decided she would ignore him and spend an enjoyable evening with her friends.

She pulled out a party dress she had made back in Ohio. She had feared she would never wear it but—here was an occasion after all. She adjusted the neckline and twirled before her mirror. The thin green fabric set off the sable thickness of her coronet of curls. About her neck she wore the gold locket her parents had given her on her eighteenth birthday. She snatched up a gossamer shawl and declared herself ready for a festive evening.

The clip-clop of hooves heralded the arrival of Boyd Hamilton in his fancy black rig.

Roarc grabbed Rian's shoulder.

"Come on, son, let's go see if the horses are penned up tonight."

"Yeah, they are, Papa. Don't you remember Mose and I did that already."

"Well—come on anyway." He led the protesting boy out the back door as Boyd Hamilton stepped up on the front porch.

Mylena's greeting was warm and friendly. Encouraged, and noticing the absence of the dour Roarc, Boyd was effusive in his compliments on her appearance. She was a beauty!

Soon she was settled in the buggy and they were tooling along toward town.

It seemed the entire town had turned out for the wedding in the small white church at sunset. Mylena and Boyd were seated near the front as vows were exchanged by the happy couple.

Dr. Sims was well-liked and so his choice of a new wife was accepted with pleasure.

A reception was held in the hotel dining room while a dance floor had been erected just outside in the street. Musicians tuned up their instruments as wedding cake was being served inside. Nora Davis had outdone herself in decorating and preparing for the festivities.

In the mood for a fun evening, Mylena enjoyed the dancing. Boyd was a dashing partner as he knew all the latest steps. She didn't lack for partners all night but he seemed to claim most of her dances. Her smiling face, along with her green dress, were magnets of attraction.

In the shadows Laredo watched. No, he didn't want to dance with Mylena. He wanted to do much more than that . . . .

As the evening waned and the musicians wound down, people began to scatter to their homes or wagons. Boyd escorted Mylena to his fancy black rig and began the drive back to the Rhynhart ranch.

Laredo followed.

CHAPTER 10

Boyd was an exemplary companion. His stories of living back in Boston quite fascinated Mylena as they rolled along. He slowed the buggy until they were barely moving thus prolonging the evening.

At a point midway home, the pair heard galloping hooves overtaking their rig. Boyd looked around casually to find a lone rider bearing down on them. Passing them, the rider grabbed the harness of Boyd's horse to stop him. Boyd yelled.

"Hey! What are you doing?"

But the mysterious rider swung a hard arm and knocked Boyd from the buggy to the ground. Then he was off his own horse and beating Boyd unmercifully.

It was the hated Laredo.

Mylena recognized him immediately. She grabbed the buggy whip from its socket and flipped a fast thwack at the intruder. It caught him across the face cutting him from eye to chin. She flipped the whip again and he fell to the ground holding his face as blood dripped between his fingers.

Mylena turned the whip on the black horse. With a great lunge, the horse galloped into the night leaving the two downed men behind. She raced toward the ranch. What if Laredo followed and pulled her from the buggy as well? She was scared within an inch of her life. If he caught her . . . .

Roarc was sitting on the bunkhouse porch with the men. He had endured a miserable evening and he couldn't decide quite why. Sudden sounds of hoof beats sent a shaft of alarm through Roarc. If Mylena had been home where she belonged he wouldn't have been so worried . . . .

"What in thunder?" Mose began as Roarc signaled for silence. The cadence of hooves came closer until the black buggy and horse loomed into sight.

Mylena had a hard time stopping the frightened animal but she finally succeeded leaving it's black sides heaving.

"Mylena, what happened?" Roarc was beside her now trying to calm her as she stammered for words to explain. Her hair had tumbled about her face and she was disheveled in general.

She stumbled from the buggy into his arms.

"It's Laredo! He's after Boyd. Come quick! He may have killed him!"

"Saddle up, men!" called Roarc. "Bring your guns!"

He swept Mylena back into the buggy, took the reins and turned the exhausted horse around. He finally urged the animal to begin the journey back to the site of their confrontation.

They scanned the countryside for a sight of Laredo—but he seemed to have disappeared.

At last, in the darkness, they spied Boyd still lying beside the road.

"Oh, I hope he isn't dead!" Mylena moaned as she jumped from the buggy.

Soon Roarc was assessing the man's injuries. He was in a lot of pain but he was lucid.

"I think his leg is broken. We need some kind of splint so we can move him back to town."

The other cow hands appeared. Within minutes, a stout stick had been located and Boyd's leg tied snugly to it with rope. He moaned in pain. Gently they moved him to the buggy. Mylena held him as Roarc drove back to Callahan.

There was still a light in Dr. Sims' house as the group rode into town. The hub-bub attracted the doctor's attention. He came to the door immediately as he was quite used to being disturbed after dark. But on his wedding night? He grinned to himself—oh well!

Carefully the cow hands lifted the injured victim into the doctor's inner sanctum where all was still and white. After an examination, his leg was set, splinted and a large dose of whiskey was prescribed for pain. His cuts and bruises were tended as he was settled for the night.

"One of you better go wake his father and tell him what has happened." Roarc urged the waiting cowboys. "The rest of you high-tail it back to the ranch. Laredo may be stalking us all in the dark. Be careful!"

Mylena remembered the look of hatred in Laredo's eyes as he stared up at her through the blood dripping from his face. She didn't think he'd be doing much more stalking tonight. He would be needing medical attention himself if she had seen his face correctly.

Leaving Boyd in the doctor's hands and with his father coming immediately, Roarc called to his men.

"Wait up! We'll ride back together. But watch out for Laredo!"

As they rode along, he glanced at Mylena. She began to re-do her hair to make herself a bit more presentable.

"Did Laredo touch you, Mylena?" He would kill him if he did!

"No. I hit him with the whip a couple of times. He fell and then I whipped the horse and came running home."

"Since when have you become so adept with a whip, lady?" Roarc couldn't help grinning at his imagining her wielding the offending weapon.

"Oh my brother taught me. We used to have contests to see who was the fastest with a whip when we were kids at home. It can be pretty deadly."

"Lady, you are full of surprises!" He couldn't help the laugh that bubbled up from his throat despite the seriousness of the evening's happenings. He was more thankful than he could say to have her safe beside him.

Once back at the ranch, he tossed the reins to China.

"Stable this rig until tomorrow. We'll return it then. See about the horse; he must be exhausted."

He led Mylena from the buggy and walked her to the door. He couldn't seem to let her go. He kept wanting to touch her, to know she was all right.

She turned at her bedroom door. Her blue eyes were enormous in her pale face.

"Oh Roarc, I'm so glad you came. I was so scared!"

He took her in his arms once more—just to hold her—just to know she was fine.

"I know. Get some rest now. It's all over." He pressed a soft kiss on her brow and let her go—reluctantly.

Mylena felt guilty for Boyd's accident. Now he was laid up at home with a leg in traction and three broken ribs as well. He was lucky they hadn't damaged him more bringing him in to the doctor that awful night. Each Saturday now she insisted on visiting him in town. Sometimes they all went in the wagon to shop; sometimes only Mose and China accompanied her in the buggy. Roarc was adamant that she not be out alone or with only one companion. Sometimes she felt a bit stifled but Mose counseled her that Roarc was just concerned about her safety.

She often watched Roarc for some sign that he had been affected by their kiss in the moonlight. But he remained stoical and silent. When he came near her, she always felt herself melting. She wondered if that feeling would ever go away. It only seemed to intensify as time went on.

Laredo looked at his face in the wavy mirror of the bunkhouse at Chidister's place. He had an ugly scar that ran from just below his left eye all the way to his chin. He was more than angry. He had grown to hate Mylena Harris. She was the one who had inflicted that injury on him. Now even the girls in the saloons looked away when he came near.

He really should have gone to town to Dr. Sims to have the gash stitched up—but he had been afraid old man Hamilton would have him jailed for injuring his son. He and Satch had heard there was a warrant out for their arrest. They had been camping out in various locations each night. It was getting old. Laredo had slipped back into the bunkhouse at Chidister's to take a look at his face. Meanwhile his hate festered for Mylena and also for Roarc Rhynhart. Sooner or later he would find a way to pay them back he vowed.

The local newspaper, published every two weeks, declared the town was getting a library thanks to Roland Hamilton. A new librarian was due in a fortnight. Townspeople were excited. Boyd was especially glad as he had read everything he could get his hands on already. He was bored beyond belief. The only bright spot in the week was Mylena's visit on Saturday.

Four weeks after his accident, he was able to hobble around the house when Mylena came to visit. They sat in the parlor and sipped tea. He decided the time had come to ask Mylena to be his wife. The weather was cooling off in preparation for the winter months. Soon she would not be able to visit every week. If they were married, she would be here with him all the time.

Confident of her answer, he took her hand as they sat on the horsehair sofa in his parent's parlor. She had never let him do more than hold her hand but he still felt she was in love with him. How could she not be? He was the most eligible bachelor in town.

"Mylena, I think it's time we announced our engagement and planned our wedding for an early date before the holidays. Do you have a preference as to when?"

"What?" Mylena jumped up and faced him with shock written all over her face.

He smiled. "You heard me, you little minx. I want to marry you—and soon."

This was not the most romantic proposal she had ever heard but it was certainly the most surprising. She had only meant her visits to display friendship—not romance. She couldn't believe he was serious. She swallowed convulsively and sat back down tracing a finger along the tapestry of the sofa cushion.

"Boyd, you don't want to marry me. I'm not in love with you. You deserve a woman who loves you to distraction. Somewhere out there—there is one who will. But it isn't me. Remember I've been married and I know."

"Yes, you do! You love me! You come to see me constantly. If you didn't love me, you wouldn't do that." He argued as she shook her head in denial.

"I come out of friendship. I feel so sad about your accident. Perhaps I feel guilty, I don't know. But that isn't enough for a marriage. I've been in one like that and I don't want another."

Their afternoon visit was ruined. Boyd became petulant while Mylena remained a bit shocked. She was sorry she had led the man on to think she might be seriously in love with him.

She cut her visit short and left him in a bad humor. He certainly didn't take defeat well!

Mose found Mylena sitting in the buggy sniffling. He pulled out his pocket watch. It was far too early to go home at their usual time.

"Little Missy, what's wrong?" He shuffled up to the buggy to ask quietly.

Startled, Mylena swiped her eyes with a handkerchief and whispered as if anyone nearby could hear. "Could we go home early?"

"Why shore. Let me get China from the livery stable and we'll be off." Fortunately Rian had been visiting the Grady boys that day and had not come with them to town.

Clip-clopping along the road, Mylena's silence unnerved Mose. He had never seen her like this. He shot her a quick glance, then decided to ask.

"Everything all right with Hamilton?"

"Yes. Fine."

"Louise doing all right?"

"Yes."

"Then what in tarnation is wrong with you?" he growled.

"He asked me to marry him! And that ruined everything!" she wailed.

"Who asked you? Hamilton?"

"Ye-e-e-s," she answered tearfully.

"Then why did that ruin anything?" Mose was puzzled.

"Because I'm not in love with HIM!" Mylena blubbered into her handkerchief.

"Ohhhh." Mose immediately understood. Wrong man had asked he suspected.

There was little else to say as they drove along. By the time they arrived at the ranch Mylena had control of her emotions. She hopped from the wagon with a quiet "thank you" and made for the house with her few purchases.

Mose unhitched the buggy near the barn as Roarc emerged nearby. He was nailing some boards on the work wagon making the sides higher to hold more of the wheat they would be harvesting soon.

"You're back early."

"Yep."

"Anything wrong?"

"Nope."

"Well—what?" He stopped with his hands on his hips.

"If you wanta know any more, just ask Mylena." Mose growled as he tossed the reins atop the harness and made for the bunkhouse. Those two were idiots! Anybody with two eyes could see they were made for each other. Anybody but them! Oh well, he wasn't hired to play Cupid so there was nothing he could do. He took off for the bunkhouse where he pulled down the huge iron skillet and prepared to fry a few "potaters" for supper.

Mylena was unusually quiet as Roarc sat down to supper. Rian was back with tales of his day with the Gradys. Throughout all his chatter Roarc kept glancing at Mylena's pale face. It looked like she had been crying. Her eyes were decidedly pink.

He waited until Rian went out to feed the dogs before he asked quietly, "Everything going well in town today?"

"Yes, fine." Her answer was short as she rose to clear the table.

"Hamilton still recuperating well?"

"Yes."

He gave up. He took his pipe from the mantle and went to sit on the front porch. She sometimes joined him there in the evenings. Perhaps she would come out and tell him what was wrong. He hoped so. It worried him to have her upset.

But she didn't. As soon as the dishes were washed and put away, Mylena went directly to her room, prepared for bed and lay down. Boyd's proposal had ended their friendship, she knew. She had been so concerned about his injury, due to her, that she had been far too caring. She had never meant to do that. If only it had been Roarc asking . . . . tears fell onto her pillow.

Opening the new library had taken precedence over everything else in Callahan for two weeks. A new librarian had arrived fresh from the city. She was tall, slim and red-headed with huge gray eyes—quite a beauty. She had taken rooms in the boarding house and settled in very nicely.

It was two weeks before Mylena agreed to go into town again. This time she went only to help in buying foodstuff for the coming month. The men seemed to depend on her decisions more and more lately. Once that chore was taken care of, she decided to visit the new library.

The room was large and book lined. Mylena was enchanted with the selection of books displayed. There was also a table bearing newspapers from Denver, from Colorado Springs and even from Pueblo. She was impressed.

A young lady appeared from around the back of a bookshelf with an arm load of books.

"Oh, hello! I didn't know you were here. I'm the new librarian, Edna Carlyle."

Mylena was happy to meet the young woman and an instant friendship grew between the pair. Before she knew it, Mylena had spent an hour visiting. Then she had an idea.

"I have a friend who had an accident and is home-bound for a while. He needs something new to read but he cannot come to select something. I wonder, if I chose a few books for him, could you deliver them to his house?"

"I'm sure I could. Where does he live?"

"In the big house at the end of Mercer Road. You can't miss it."

"Oh yes, I've seen it. It's almost a mansion." Edna laughed happily. She looked forward to seeing the inside of that three-story house.

Mylena selected four books on completely different subjects, signed her name on a library card, and thanked Edna for agreeing to make the delivery. It was time to meet the men for the trip home. She had no more time to visit either Boyd or Louise—but she was happy with her afternoon.

Immediately after supper, Edna Carlyle donned her gray hat and cape, gathered the books Mylena had chosen and walked up the street. She turned the corner and eyed the mansion at the end of the cul-d-sac. She straightened her back and marched on. The man was probably some old codger who had fallen down the stairs so she would smile and make the delivery as quickly as possible.

She lifted the brass knocker and was surprised to be greeted by a tiny, bird-like lady with pale hair. Edna introduced herself and explained her mission.

"Oh, do come in. I'm Mrs. Roland Hamilton and you are to see my son, Boyd. He had a bad accident recently. He's in the reading room. Come right in. He will enjoy some company."

Edna was astounded as she spied the handsome young man rising on his crutches to meet her. Almost tongue-tied with surprise, she finally blurted out her reason for being there. He took the package of books and glanced through them, then smiled.

"Mylena has good taste. I will enjoy all of these. Please sit down Miss . . . uh . . . . " He gestured toward a chair nearby. Edna sank into it thankfully. Her knees felt a bit wobbly.

"You did say 'Miss' Edna Carlyle, didn't you?" Boyd eyed the lovely young woman seated before him. She was dressed all in gray but the glorious red of her hair offset the dull color of her dress. "Where are you from?"

"Philadelphia. I'm from the city so this a very new experience for me."

"Well, well—we must see that it is a very enjoyable one for you. I've just spent six months back in Boston at a banking seminar. I rather miss the city myself."

Their friendship was off to an auspicious start.

CHAPTER 11

While Clint and Walt were gone to Kansas City with the cattle, Mose and Roarc were assigned to exercise Princess and her colt, now called Rocket. Every afternoon they took them out for a ride, then exercised them in the corral. Mylena and Rian often came down to watch. As Rian sat on the top rail of the wooden fence, Mylena leaned on the sides watching.

"What I wouldn't give for a ride on Princess," muttered Mylena as she eyed the graceful mare making her rounds of the corral.

"Papa! Miss Mylena wants to ride Princess!" Rian's shrill little voice echoed around the area.

"Shh, Rian!" Mylena adjured the little boy to keep quiet. She wasn't here to ride horses after all. She had been hired to cook and keep house—and maybe teach Rian a few things.

Roarc came to the fence where they were watching.

"She does? Can you ride, Mylena?"

"Of course I can ride. After all I'm a country girl." She laughed as she answered.

"All right, tomorrow evening we'll take a ride out to the west windmill. I need to check on the water level in the tank there anyway."

"Can I go too, Papa? Can I?" Rian was not about to be put off.

"Sure, son, you can ride Paint Pony."

"Oh boy! I'll be a real cowboy!" Rian jumped from the fence and hopped about in glee.

Roarc turned to Mylena.

"Do you have riding clothes?"

"Yes, I packed them in the bottom of my trunk just in case I might need them out here in the west." Her smile was incandescent.

"Then we'll go." He turned as Mose called out something across the corral.

The day was unending as Mylena waited for the time to come when she would again be on a horse for a ride through the evening. She baked a huge cherry cobbler from a jar she had bought at Mr. Dickens store; then she stirred up a large pot of stew in case they came in hungry after their ride.

She unearthed her riding habit from the bowels of her trunk. She had even included her boots and a hat, crumpled now from being packed so long in the crowded space. She shook them all out and decided they would have to do. She was going!

At last Rian came running to the back door.

"Miss Mylena, it's time to go riding. Are you ready? Papa is waiting."

Those were the magic words for her.

"Yes I am! Let's go!"

Mylena hurriedly followed Rian to the barn. Roarc was adjusting the girth of Arrow's saddle while Princess stood aside with ears pricked up. Mose saw Rian securely atop Paint Pony as Mylena approached Princess. She quietly handed her two lumps of sugar—just to be friends. Princess chomped them up immediately, then looked at Mylena for more snuffling her inquisitively.

"That's all, pretty lady. At least for now." Mylena's laughter rang out as she gathered up the reins and prepared to mount.

Roarc moved to hold the mare's head as Mylena slid into the saddle. No problems arose as the two seemed to meld their friendship. Mylena's hair, braided into a long sable plait, hung down beneath her wilted hat as she jauntily nudged the horse forward.

Soon Roarc was mounted as well and leading the way across the pasture as the evening breeze ruffled the collar or Mylena's blouse. He watched her stealthily checking her ability to control the spirited horse. She had been correct. She really could ride.

He rode along beside her for a while, then turned to ask, "Where did you learn to ride so well, young lady. You've been holding out on us."

"No, I haven't. You just never asked if I could ride." Mylena's saucy answer put a grin on Roarc's handsome face. She always had a pert come back.

"Did you and Will ride a lot?"

"Heavens no. Will was not fond of horses. Sometimes I thought they weren't fond of him either. He was thrown several times but fortunately his beloved banjo was never damaged."

She laughed softly remembering. He had been very cautious around horses and had never been seriously injured at all.

"My brother was the horseman. He was exceptional. I often wonder what he would have become if he hadn't been killed at Shiloh. My father never got over losing him."

"Look, Papa! There's a coyote!" Rian's excited exclamation interrupted their conversation. A buff colored animal slipped quickly out of sight in the long grass.

Roarc looked about with knowing eyes.

"We'd better pick up our pace. It's still a distance to the windmill and we don't want to be out here after dark."

Rian's Paint Pony seemed to take four steps to the other horses' two. He was tired by the time they arrived at the whirling windmill. The horses drank from the tank thirstily as Roarc produced a tin cup and poured cold water from the spigot of the windmill for each of them. The tanks water level proved to be high so there were no worries here. Apparently the vandals had not disturbed this area—at least not yet.

Mylena and Roarc sat talking peacefully while Rian hopped about picking a few late blooming flowers for Mylena. The horses grazed in the sweet green grass surrounding the tank. At last it was time to saddle up once more for the ride home. On a rise before they arrived at the ranch corrals, Roarc stopped his horse, took Mylena's reins and pointed behind them.

"Look. You won't see anything like that back East."

Mylena swung around in her saddle. She was facing the most spectacular sunset she had ever seen. Orange and coral clouds silhouetted the blue rick rack of mountains. Golden shafts of sunlight speared the entire view. She caught her breath. Roarc was right.

After a few seconds, as the scene changed minute by minute, she smiled up at him.

"You really love this country, don't you?"

He looked off into the distance before he answered. Then, slowly, he replied.

"Yes, I do. I love the wide-openness—the fresh air—and not having to swipe down trees to see where I'm going."

Mylena's laugh rang out once more. "I understand!" Then she was off loping toward the corral and the waiting Mose.

Rian was the first to ride back into the corral. Mose had him down and Paint Pony unsaddled by the time the other two rode in.

"Shall I take care of Princess—or shall I set supper on the table?"

"Supper, Miss Mylena! I'm hungry!" Rian settled that with alacrity.

Roarc laughed and waved the two off. He was hungry too—for more than just food.

On a clear day with a brisk wind blowing, Clint and Walt rode in. Much back-slapping and hoorahing took place in the bunkhouse that evening. They had returned by train bringing their horses back as well as payment for Roarc's cattle. Each man received a portion of that payment for each of them had worked hard herding, branding, dehorning, castrating, worming and rounding-up the cattle in general.

Clint and Walt had decided to go down to Texas for the winter months but they would be back in early spring. Roarc had described their bitter winters to Mylena. She couldn't imagine snow so deep they couldn't see the tops of their buildings sometimes. He had told her how they tied ropes from one building to another in order to find their way between chores during the worst snows. He had described how one older neighbor had frozen to death between the barn and the house one winter because he lost his way in the blinding whiteness. She shuddered at the thought.

When cold weather arrived, they would butcher all the hogs; the chickens would be sold to restaurants in Colorado Springs and shipped there by rail. They would keep only a few, for food and eggs, in the warm barn during the winter months. Almost all the cattle had been sold in Kansas City so only a small herd would be kept for milk and meat until spring when hogs and cattle, chickens and sheep were again bought to be raised during the summer and sold in the fall.

Mylena listened to all these plans as her days spun out preparing the house for winter as well. She had asked permission to sew new curtains for the entire house. Roarc, surprised, for he hadn't missed having curtains, agreed. Mylena had spent two days with Vera Grady sewing on her sewing machine. Vera always had some mending to be done so she was always happy to have Mylena come for a few days. Their baby girl was growing by leaps and bounds. It was difficult to remember that she had been so tiny at birth. The boys had called her "Bitsy" and she still bore that name.

Back at the ranch, Mylena hung the new curtains, then stood back with a wide smile.

They were full with enough material to be closed during cold weather thus insulating their rooms a bit.

Roarc was quite pleased when she explained this to him.

Not too much wood was available on these eastern plains. Many people used buffalo chips for fuel. At one time, herds of buffalo dotted the area leaving their mark on the landscape.

Roarc ordered several cords of wood from Colorado Springs to tide them over the winter months.

Clint and Walt brought back gifts for everyone. Mose received a new brand of tobacco. He couldn't decide if he liked it or not. China and Sim got bottles of whiskey much to their delight.

Roarc's memento was a new wallet. He laughed long and loud as he tossed his old worn one away.

"You boys knew just what I needed!"

Rian opened his cardboard box to find a tin music box that played a lilting tune. He was fascinated by it. He had to go play it for Olga and for Paint Pony as well as for Princess and Rocket. The tinny music ricocheted around the barn.

The boys bashfully presented Mylena a package as well. Upon opening it, she found a new shawl woven with the colors of the sunset she and Roarc had watched. She was enchanted and thanked them profusely. It was a happy homecoming for all.

Boyd Hamilton could walk around town on his crutches now. He seemed to spend a lot of time at the library. He and Miss Edna, as she was known by the local folks, could be seen dining at the hotel dining room quite often.

Laredo and Satch were still hiding out in different camping spots in the area. The weather was cooling and Satch was getting itchy feet.

"I'm tired of this living on the land, Laredo. I'm ready to move on. We're not doing any good here."

"NO! You idiot! Don't you know I'm not finished here yet?" Laredo snarled as he lit a cigarette with a long flaming ember from their campfire.

"I'm not leaving 'til I'm through." He had been devising methods of destruction for the Rhynhart ranch but nothing really seemed right to him just yet.

"If you wanta go, GO." He was tired of baby-sitting the whining cow hand anyway.

The next morning, when Laredo awoke, Satch had disappeared with all his gear.

"Well if he wants to risk getting arrested, let him!"

But it was lonely living alone hand to mouth out here in the sticks of civilization. His mood darkened daily as he mulled ideas for revenge.

For several days dark blue clouds had shrouded the mountains to the west. Roarc eyed them suspiciously. They did not need rain right now. He hoped those clouds would stay over the mountains until they could harvest their wheat.

However, each day the clouds seemed to hover closer and closer. No rain fell on their land but the men watched anxiously.

Mylena was upset. Was it time for her to make a move from the ranch? Wheat harvest would take several weeks—then it would be time to butcher hogs. There was no way she could leave them all in the lurch with so much work ahead to do. Besides, where would she go next? It would have to be some place where she didn't meet Roarc every now and then.

Perhaps she might find something to do in Colorado Springs. But oh she would miss little Rian as well as Mose with his unending supply of tales and advice.

Roarc had closed the loft. He had moved the table and lamp into the new bedroom where he and Rian had now taken up residence. The new bed took some getting used to after a summer spent sleeping on a feather bed in the loft. But the loft would soon be far too cold for sleeping. He was thankful they had taken the time to build the new bedroom. The only problem for Roarc was thinking of Mylena sleeping just on the other side of the wall. This seemed to bother him a lot.

He would never admit it but he could not imagine life without finding her in the house, lamps aglow, every evening when he came in tired and hungry. He looked forward to hearing her soft voice guiding Rian with his reading and numbers. She was so different from Lavina. Could he possibly carve out a life with Mylena? He was beginning to think of that—a lot.

One blustery evening, the wind began to blow a gale. Mylena looked out to find dark blue clouds ringing the sky. Rumbles of thunder echoed across the plains. She took a pan of cornbread out of the oven and moved to the back door Where was Rian?

She stepped out on the back porch calling for him. No answer. She moved down the path toward the barn. If he was busy with Paint Pony, he would never hear the storm blowing up.

Chickens with their feathers blowing enough to show their nude skin ran in the direction of the chicken house. Mylena stopped to slam shut the door securing them for the night.

The wind was growing in strength. A streak of lightening zig-zagged across the sky as a tremendous boom of thunder followed. Mylena, scared and shaking now, grabbed open the barn door and sagged inside. Several more streaks of lightening sizzled through the air. Thunder followed loud enough to wake the dead. Mylena was terrified. The dark barn enclosed her in a world of memories that sent her into a frenzy of fear. Small moans of alarm seemed to come from her throat whether she wanted them to or not. She was shaking uncontrollably.

Roarc snapped shut the gate of Arrow's stall. He didn't want his horses out in this weather. They were all now securely sheltered for the night. Suddenly he heard a sound. It was not something he recognized. What was it? Olga gave a short bark but he quieted her with a gesture of one hand.

He moved through the gloom toward the barn door. Shocked, he found Mylena sagged down weeping hysterically. He lifted her and placed his arms about her.

"Hey, it's all right," he soothed.

It took a few minutes before she recognized him. Then she grasped him about his waist and held on for dear life. She was sobbing uncontrollably.

"Honey, what is it? What's wrong?" Alarmed, he could not seem to quiet her.

She couldn't answer. She could only gasp for breath as she tried to speak.

"Th-th-th—s-t-o-r-m . . . . "

"Shhh—it'll be over soon." He smoothed her hair as he spoke softly.

"N-o-o . . . . " she wailed.

"Haven't you been in a storm before?"

"Y-e-s . . . . No . . . . " She was hysterical.

"When? Tell me." He rubbed her back as he spoke softly.

"Once—when I was a little girl . . . . Ohhh!" She quaked as another bolt of lightening and a boom of thunder rocked the barn.

He held her head against his chest as the rumble of his voice penetrated her thoughts.

"Tell me about it."

"It was a tornado I think. My grandmother was running to the cellar where we were. She couldn't run fast and my uncle went out to help her." She stopped to swallow a sob.

"Then what happened?"

"Some boards blew off the windmill and hit them both in the head—killing them."

"Oh, honey, I'm sorry. But we're safe here in this big old barn."

Mylena raised her tear soaked face. "Are you sure?"

Roarc could no longer help himself. He lowered his mouth to hers in a kiss that took her breath away. She could no longer hear the storm outside. She could only feel the storm raging inside her body. Mylena had never before understood how a woman could be carried away by a man in the throes of passion. The romance novels always wrote about it—but now she knew.

Roarc's mouth ravaged Mylena's in sweet desire. All the love she had stored so carefully now for weeks came soaring through. She responded as if she had never known there was a storm outside at all.

At last he lifted his lips from hers. Her eyes were pools of blue in the dimness. He started to say something, then lowered his mouth to hers again as the fire that engulfed them surged once more.

He didn't want to release her. She felt just right in his arms. He always knew she would; he just wouldn't admit it even to himself. Now he held her close as the wind howled around the barn, as the horses snuffled in their hay, as Olga sniffed their feet, then ambled back to her bed.

Calm now, Mylena suddenly realized where she was, what she was doing. She raised shocked eyes to Roarc's face in the semi-darkness.

"Oh, Roarc, I'm sorry! I didn't mean to . . . . " her voice trailed off as she spun away and ran for the barn door. In his surprise, he let her go. She grabbed open the door and fled into the rain.

"No, Mylena! Stop! Come back!" But he couldn't catch her. He could barely see her as she ran through the sheets of rain to the house.

He dashed out after her. The wind and rain were fierce. He expected to find her fallen on the ground at any moment. But she had made it inside. She stood dripping in a pool of water before the fireplace. She seemed lost and disoriented.

"You must get out of those clothes, Mylena. You're soaking wet. You'll catch pneumonia." That was the one thing he was terrified of.

She simply stood there as if she had not heard him.

He scooped her up and carried her to the bedroom. Setting her down, she was still unresponsive in shock. He began to unbutton her dress and slip it down her arms. She was soaked through. He lifted one leg, then another until she was free of the clinging garment. He sat her on the bed and removed her muddy shoes. Her chemise was soaked as well.

"Mylena, we have to get this off. Can you help me?"

She nodded her head but did not respond. He unbuttoned the offending garment, turned her around and lifted it from her torso. He found her nightgown hanging behind the door. He dragged it over her head, then laid her back down on the bed. She was completely unresponsive.

He scooped his hands to her waist beneath the nightgown and undid her damp undergarments. Her stockings came down as well. Good! He was almost through. This was hard on a man!

Once she was undressed, he slung back the quilt on her bed, shifted her under the covers and cuddled her there for a moment. Then he realized he, too, was soaking wet.

He made quick work of changing into dry clothes, then went back to check on Mylena.

She lay sleeping in her bed. It had been a difficult time for her.

He built up the fire in the fireplace and sat rocking before it. He had some thinking to do.

Mose and Rian found him there smoking before the fire. He never smoked in the house and they were surprised.

"Papa, where's Mylena? I spent all the storm in the bunkhouse playing checkers. Did you get wet outside, Papa?"

Mose was concerned about Mylena. "Where is she?" he softly asked Roarc.

"She's sleeping. She was just about drowned out in the rain. I insisted she go to bed before she caught pneumonia."

"Ummhmm." Mose sensed something peculiar in the air.

It took several days for the wheat to dry out enough to harvest. Roarc and Mylena spent no time together. It was as if each of them was embarrassed when they remembered the interlude in the barn. Besides, Mylena wondered just how she had gotten undressed and in bed that day. Roarc seemed as taciturn as ever and she didn't dare ask. But she remembered the fire of his kisses . . . .

One evening as Rian set a basket of fresh eggs on the table, Roarc looked up from the whet stone he was using to sharpen his knife.

"I see you don't seem afraid of that white rooster any more. Did you finally make friends with him?"

Rian looked at Mylena. She winked at him and grinned.

"I guess so, Papa." Then he went whistling back outside with a matching grin on his face.

CHAPTER 12

Laredo sat coiling rope in Chidister's lean-to shed. The cowhands were all in the bunkhouse eating supper. He had bought a brand-new rope in town to replace the frayed one he was taking from Chidister. He had finally come up with a plan to destroy all the people at the Rhynhart ranch. He smiled in recollection of his devious plan. He had three cans of kerosene already stashed away behind the tool shed. They were hidden in some tall weeds just waiting.

The terrible scar on his face pulled as he smiled. His hatred for Mylena speared through him as he massaged the puckered skin.

He had overheard Grady talking to Chidister yesterday. Roarc was planning to begin harvesting his wheat tomorrow. Grady was planning to help. Now was the perfect time for his move.

His furtive movements around Chidister's ranch had kept him in touch with what was happening.

Late in the evening he removed the coils of frayed rope he had left soaking in a tub of kerosene. He rolled them in tow sacks and tied them to his saddle. They were heavy but he thought he could do it. The time was right. He made sure he had a supply of matches tucked away in his vest pocket. He even had a flask of kerosene in case he needed it.

Surreptitiously he untied his horse and plodded away toward town. He didn't want anyone to follow his moves. A few miles along, he changed direction and headed for Roarc's ranch. If they were planning to start harvesting tomorrow, they would all be home getting ready.

He rode along the back edge of the wheat field. The stalks were dry and ready to be cut. Just right! He slipped from his horse and unrolled the kerosene soaked rope. It was so heavy his horse had objected a bit as he had ridden along. Laredo stroked his chin wondering just where the best place would be to start the fire.

He decided to walk a few rows down, string the soaked rope all the way across one row and then set fire to the rope. Once afire it would burn the entire wheat field to a cinder. Then, it should catch the outbuildings and maybe even the barn where Roarc kept his fine horses. If he was lucky, it would also burn the house where Mylena reigned. He smiled an evil smile as he thought of all the destruction he would cause. He stooped down and lit the end of the oily rope. It sizzled and caught fire as the flames rushed all the way along the rope. Soon the entire wheat field was ablaze.

Laredo watched in glee. It would be a while before they discovered what was happening he felt sure. He stood and watched for long moments. At last he decided to move one coil of the rope to another location. It was still soaked and ready.

However, as he turned, he caught his boot in the coil. Arms waving wildly, he fell headlong to the ground. The movement of the rope sent flames shooting back up to coil around his boot. He rolled over and began to slap at the flames before they caught his britches on fire. Too late he realized he had nothing to fight the flames with—only his kerosene soaked gloves. He shrugged out of his vest and slapped at the fire engulfing him. He had forgotten he had a supply of matches stashed inside the vest pockets. At their contact with the flames, they began to ignite. He was caught in an inferno of his own making. He screamed but there was no one near enough to hear his anguish.

"Boss! Hey, Boss!" Clint's voice caught Roarc's ear as he sat eating supper. He rose at once. Clint sounded alarmed.

Roarc met him at the back door. "What is it?"

"The wheat field is on fire! You'd better come quick!"

"On fire? What do you mean?"

By now the other hands were running from the bunkhouse toward the barn.

Roarc yelled at Rian and Mylena, "Stay here!" Then he was gone following the running men. Rian ran to peek out the back door. Mylena was right behind him. Sure enough, they could see the red glow of fire all across the western edge of the ranch.

How could this have happened?

For long moments the men were too stunned to act. Then, coming to their senses, they began to make a plan. The wheat field was gone. They could never stop the fire burning there. Their main goal was to save the outbuildings and the barn. They began carrying water in buckets to douse the wood of the barn. The fire was fast and burning closer by the minute.

Smoke billowed in the evening air choking all of them. At last Mose declared they'd better let the animals out of the barn "just in case" . . . .

Rian cried as he saw Paint Pony gallop away. Princess and Rocket, followed by Arrow, were right behind him. Olga came barking to the house to stand beside Rian and Mylena.

Suddenly Mylena remembered the chickens. She ran to shoo them out. She knew they would all come back but she didn't want them to burn to death in the hen house. The hogs were on the sheltered side of the big barn. They should be safe enough in their muddy sty.

She turned around to find a sobbing Rian right behind her. She must calm him down or he might be in danger.

"Rian, listen to me. You go sit on the back porch and take care of Olga. She is going to have some more puppies and she needs you to be with her right now. Can you take care of her like a big boy?"

"Some more puppies right now?" He hiccuped as his eyes grew big.

"No, not right at this minute—later on. Can you take care of her?"

He nodded his head and went with Mylena as she sat him down on the back porch with his arm around the black and white dog.

"Now you stay right there. I'm going to the windmill to help draw water." Matching actions to her words, she soon was pumping steadily as one man after another ran up to fill his water bucket.

Grady spotted the fire. He and his boys arrived to help. It was a harrowing time for all as they worked to save what they could of the ranch buildings. Fire crept ever closer to the barn. It destroyed the privy and one of the clothes line poles Roarc had erected at Mylena's request.

The house seemed safe enough if the wind didn't blow. Luckily it was a fairly calm evening.

Roarc had the men chop the wooden fence away from the barn. Some of it was already afire. But the barn itself remained intact thanks to the diligence of the workmen.

Hours later the men began to trail in from the destruction. Charred ground surrounded the entire west side of their homestead. But the big old barn was still standing.

As the men gathered discussing the awful sight Mylena missed Roarc. Sooty and smokey from her time pumping at the windmill, she thankfully entered the kitchen. The house had been spared. She made a big pot of coffee and called to them. They could barely move they were so exhausted.

Looking around, she spotted everyone except Roarc. Where was he?

Grady spoke at just that moment.

"We found a dead body near the back of the wheat field . . . . burned so bad you could hardly recognize him." Then he looked around and spied Mylena listening. Her face was as white as a sheet beneath the soot and grime.

"Roarc?" she gasped. She began to run toward the barn in a frenzy of fear. Had Roarc burned to death? Was he gone? She began to cry as she ran toward the smoke blackened barn.

"Mylena! Come back here!" Mose rose to call her but she paid him no mind. She ran on toward the charred fence of the barn.

Suddenly Roarc came from inside the building. His shirt was burned almost off his body. His britches were scorched and his hair was disheveled. His face was covered with soot and grime but he had never looked so handsome to Mylena.

She ran to him. Tears flooded her face as she looked up at him.

"Oh, Roarc, I thought you were dead . . . . "

He folded her tightly in his arms.

"Not hardly, honey. It's been quite a night but we're all still together. That's all that matters." He kissed her soot and all. She gladly returned his kisses with a fire of her own.

Mose put his hands on his hips and grunted.

"Well finally."

Roarc kept his arm about Mylena as they returned to the house. Someone had set the fire. Would they come back? Grady and his boys were to sleep beside the windmill in their wagon while China chose to sleep in his bedroll beneath it. Hopefully they would watch in case the culprit returned. Everyone was so tired it was doubtful they would awaken. However, everyone was also sleeping with anxiety so perhaps they would hear any strange noise after all. Nothing more could be done until daylight.

Mylena provided hot water for Roarc to wash up on the back porch while she used the pitcher and bowl in her own room. Wrapped in a flannel robe, she ventured out her bedroom door when she heard Roarc enter the house at last.

"Is everyone settling down for a while?"

"Yes. I put Rian to bed in his dirty clothes. We'll clean him up tomorrow. He was too tired to bathe tonight—or should I say this morning?"

Mylena smiled sleepily as Roarc took her in his arms once more. He laid a bronzed cheek against her softer one. His was bristly with his nights beard. But Mylena didn't notice. She was too thankful to be held in his arms—safely and lovingly at last.

"We'll talk tomorrow. We're too tired to think right now. But I want you to know how glad I am you're here with me—not just for this disaster—but for all time. I want you for my wife. I love you Mylena." He sealed his words with a long kiss.

Too happy to talk Mylena nodded her tired head and slipped into her room—and sleep.

Day break found them all up and anxious to find out what had happened to cause the awful destruction of Roarc's wheat field and almost his home. First of all, Roarc dispatched China to ride for the sheriff in town. Grady took his boys home but declared he would be back with his wagon as quickly as he could. He knew they would need help in cleaning up the charred debris.

Roarc cautioned all hands to stay away from the body they thought they had found at the back of the wheat field. As soon as the sheriff arrived, they would move to find out who it might be.

Roarc had a strong suspicion but he kept his own counsel.

Mose was full of expletives and suggestions of his own.

Sheriff Gilless was there in record time along with a deputy. China had made good time riding to town. All the men gathered at the back of the wheat field in anticipation. Who could the victim be?

A quick examination of the charred body was inconclusive. Abruptly Sim stepped forward.

"See that belt buckle? It didn't completely burn. That's Laredo's. He wore it all the time. "

"You sure?" The sheriff questioned.

"Sure, I'm sure. I rode with him while he worked for us here. I know!"

The deputy walked through the rubble behind the burned area. He carried a black hat in his hand. He handed it to the sheriff.

"This hat must have fallen off somehow. It isn't even scorched." He handed it to the sheriff.

Now Walt spoke up. "Hey, that's Laredo's hat. I'd know it anywhere. See that little medallion on the hat band? That's his, I'm sure."

"Roarc, what do you think?" The sheriff questioned as he rose, hat in hand.

"I feel sure it must be Laredo. Too many signs point to him."

The deputy was back to announce once more his findings.

"There's tracks in the dirt back here. There are horse tracks and footprints too. The horse must have run off when the fire started. No sign of him now. "

At last the charred body was wrapped in a tarp and transported back to Callahan. It would be buried in a pauper's grave in the town's cemetery. The sheriff announced the case closed due to lack of further evidence. He wondered where the other cow hand had disappeared to. But there seemed to be only one man involved in setting the fire. Well—here again—time would tell, he thought to himself. He would keep a watchful eye out for Satch as the other man was called.

Mose and China rounded up the missing cattle and horses. They had not strayed far in their panic. Princess and her foal came back the next morning.

"See, she's smarter than the average horse. She knows where her oats are!" Mose was heard to declare with laughter.

The chickens were another matter. They were scattered far and wide. Mylena and Rian spent hours catching them and returning them to their pens. But the white rooster was missing. Perhaps some animal had caught him for its breakfast.

Roarc found Arrow grazing peacefully in a far corner of the south pasture. He had enjoyed his freedom to check out any stray mares.

Neighbors came to help restore order to the Rhynhart ranch. Nothing could be done about the charred wheat field but, when it rained, things would look different there. Lumber had been hauled from town and a new corral fence completed. Mylena's clothes line had been restored as well as the new privy.

One evening Roarc completed his chores early. He headed for the house. Maybe Mylena would like to ride Princess for an outing. Before he reached the back door, he spied the black and red rig, along with the black horse, parked at the front of the house.

Anger speared through him. That supercilious Boyd Hamilton must still be trying to court Mylena. This time he would tell him what was what. He grabbed the back door with a fisted hand. But—to his surprise—not one but two extra people were sitting at the table sipping tea—TEA?

Mylena rose at once. "Oh Roarc, come in. We have company."

He stepped close and put an arm about her waist in possession.

Boyd Hamilton grinned. Just as he suspected. The rancher DID have his eye on the pretty housekeeper. No wonder he had made no time with her.

"I don't think you have met our new librarian, Miss Edna Carlyle." Mylena continued.

Roarc tipped his hat politely.

"Happy to meet you, ma'am. Hamilton, how are you?"

"Coming along nicely. I'm down to a cane now. My father suggested I drive out and take a look at the damage to your wheat crop. I thought Miss Edna might enjoy a visit with Miss Mylena so I invited her along." That should set the wily rancher at ease.

"Would you like a cup of . . . . ?" Mylena didn't finish her question as Roarc turned with a decided grin.

"Coffee, please." She always kept a pot on the back of the stove for his return to the house at any time. They settled down for a convivial visit as the evening passed pleasantly for all of them. News was exchanged from town and the story of the fire was retold.

At last Boyd suggested he take a look at the wheat field. Roarc escorted him to the back yard where the charred remains could be seen. They seemed to go on forever before their eyes.

"Will this make a difference in your ability to make your mortgage payment this year?"

Roarc rubbed his chin in thought. Was this really an official visit—or was Boyd just trying to rub in Roarc's loss? Carefully he considered his answer.

"It's a loss surely. Wheat was my main crop this year. However, with the sale of the cattle I should be able to make the payment on time."

"Very good!" Boyd was enthusiastic as they returned to the house.

Edna and Mylena enjoyed a few moments of "girl talk" as the men disappeared. Edna described her outings with Boyd in glowing terms. Mylena was thankful that he had found someone to share his time with.

She didn't feel so guilty about refusing his proposal of marriage quite so much now even though she still rued his injury.

As the men reentered the house, farewells were said all around as the pair left in a whirl of dust. Boyd reflected that Mylena was still the prettiest girl he had ever seen but she wasn't for him. Miss Edna suited him far more as she was from the city. She shared all his polished interests. He smiled to himself as they rolled along. Yes, he was quite satisfied.

Roarc returned to the house in silence. He was a bit worried. With the loss of his wheat crop a large slice of his yearly income disappeared. He would have trouble meeting his mortgage payment regardless of what he had bragged to Boyd Hamilton. He wanted desperately to marry Mylena at once but—what could he offer her if he lost the ranch?

CHAPTER 13

Roarc continued to worry as the days went by. Mylena, happy in the love they shared, went blissfully about her work. Mose watched with trepidation as the days passed with no announcement of a marriage ceremony. Those two were just right for each other—and he didn't want anything to happen to ruin things.

On Saturday as they rode to town in the wagon, Roarc turned to Mylena with a broad grin. They were to shop for supplies but he had something else on his mind as well.

"Don't you think you'd better see the dressmaker in town about a wedding dress?"

"Yes—I guess I'd better. But we haven't discussed the wedding yet."

"Just as soon as I can get my affairs in order, we'll set the date."

Mylena leaned her head against his shoulder and smiled. It couldn't come soon enough for her.

Once in town he set her down at the dressmakers shop as he had suggested. She had not met Jessie Malone, the little lady there, but they soon became friends. She displayed several bolts of fabric for Mylena to see. None of them seemed quite right. A fancy party dress was not what Mylena had in mind. That seemed a bit frivolous for life in this country setting.

"For cooler weather, perhaps I'd better have a white woolen suit. What do you think?

Then I could wear it again to church later on."

"Excellent idea! I have some material right here that might be just what you are looking for." She produced a thin woolen fabric that felt soft as a cloud.

Mylena smiled. "Yes, that's it. Now—how about a pattern?"

Decision made, Jessie took her measurements, then suggested a white taffeta lining.

Mylena chose some silver buttons and a white silk for the blouse. Satisfied at last, they parted with Jessie suggesting she visit the milliner next door for a fancy hat to complete her outfit.

As Mylena closed the door of the dressmaking salon, Louise and Dr. Sims came strolling along the boardwalk. Louise was busy stuffing some papers into her handbag. She looked up at last.

"Mylena! I didn't know you were in town!" Louise was always happy to see her friend.

"Why hello, Louise, Dr. Sims. How nice to see you. I was coming by your office in a little while—as soon as I finish my shopping."

They walked along together. Mylena paused to look into the milliners window where hats of various sizes, designs and colors were displayed.

"Oh Louise, do you have time to come in with me. I need you to help me chose a wedding hat."

"A wedding hat? Why Mylena, when?"

Mylena felt herself blushing. She recounted the fire and Roarc's asking her to be his wife shortly after. They had heard about the fire but not the details.

"How romantic!" Louise was more than pleased. Dr. Sims beamed his congratulations as well. Roarc was a fine man and well-liked in the community he knew.

"Isn't it something that we both found a new life here in Callahan, Colorado?"

"I know. I still remember how frightened we both were when we arrived here—newly widowed—no one to meet us . . . . "

Louise tucked her arm inside Dr. Sims'. Smiling up at him, she readily agreed.

"We've just been to the bank. Louise called on the real estate office the other day to ask about the land her husband had purchased. She had never looked into that. They hemmed and hawed but they finally admitted they knew she had arrived in town. After some negotiations they returned her money in exchange for the deed she held. They seemed pleased to have that land to re-sell."

Mylena put a hand to her throat. She had never thought to do that. Will had sent almost all their money here for land. She still had the deed in her trunk back at the ranch.

"If you haven't done so, why don't you look into that, Mylena? You may have some money coming too."

"Oh I certainly will. I'll talk to Roarc about doing that today."

The wedding hat was forgotten in Mylena's excitement about the land Will had bought.

She found Roarc in the livery stable and gestured for him to come outside. Surprised, he came at once. "What is it? Do you have a problem?"

"No—but let me tell you what Louise and Dr. Sims just told me." She recounted the story of their real estate visit with its subsequent settlement. Roarc was again surprised.

"You never went in and asked about the land Will had bought?"

"No—I never thought about it."

"Do you have the deed?"

"Yes, but it's back at the ranch in my trunk."

Roarc thought for a few minutes.

"There's no need to confront them without the deed in your hand. Do you know where the land is located?"

"I have no idea. I don't think Will really did either."

"Tell you what—let's come back to town next Tuesday with the deed. Their office should be open then. We'll look into this for you. You may have your money coming too."

Mylena finished her shopping for food and supplies but her mind was on the land Will had bought. Why had she never thought of looking into that before?

This was on their minds all weekend. They spoke of it quietly after Rian was in bed and they could sit by the fire and dream. Probably nothing would come of it—but it was worth looking into.

Tuesday arrived at last. They were up early and off in the buggy to Callahan. Mose agreed to keep an eye on Rian while they took care of business. They left him wailing by the front gate as they drove away. But Mose knew just how to distract him so it was not long before they were in the corral working with Princess' foal, Rocket. He was now a beauty, well trained to the bridle and docile enough to work with.

Mylena had unearthed the deed in her trunk. Upon showing it to Roarc, he frowned.

If that legal description was correct, the land described was in a poor location far north of town. He wondered if Will had been bilked. Well—they would soon know.

They left the buggy at the livery stable to walk the short distance to the real estate office. A large garish sign announced LAND FOR SALE across the front. Roarc opened the door as a fat bald man came forward gushing a welcome. Ah—new prospects he thought with a wide smile.

"Come right in! I'm Joe Collins. You are in the right place! Are you new in town?"

Roarc introduced them as the little man's feathers fell. He recognized the name "Will Harris". He had hoped never to hear from the widow—but here she was. And with a formidable companion too. Oh well—you couldn't win them all. He knew what they wanted—not that sorry block of land he felt sure. He twisted his hands anxiously.

Roarc laid out the deed, then asked about the location.

"We would like to take a look at the area if you don't mind."

Well the bald man did mind. It was a half-day ride away. He hated to close his office just for that in the middle of the week. But Roarc insisted. At last he acquiesced and agreed to ride out to show them the property.

It was a long and dusty ride. Mylena was wilted by the time they arrived at the location. It was desolate and bare. Only miles and miles of tall grass dotted with buffalo chips filled the interminable distance. Roarc checked the legal description once more. This was it.

"Mylena, you can never live out here. There's no water, no shade; you are miles from town. This is not for you. Will never saw this, did he?"

"I feel sure he didn't. He was enraptured by the advertisements so—"

Roarc flipped the ad Joe Collins had given him. Large pictures of trees and green grass decorated the folder. On the inside pictures of water filled streams teased the eye. Roarc read the entire brochure, then eyed the bald man waiting there astride his horse as they sat in the buggy.

"You know this won't do. This is false advertising. This lady needs her money back and you need the deed to this property once more."

"Oh, we can't do that . . . . " Joe Collins began. "Perhaps we might return fifty cents on the dollar but we can't refund the entire amount."

"In that case, I have a friend in the land development department in Colorado Springs. I'll telegraph him the details of this sale. Maybe he needs to look into your company and its policies."

"Oh, no, now don't do that!" Joe Collins was off his horse and standing beside the buggy now. He swiped his bald head with a handkerchief. It was hot and he was perspiring. "Let's go back to the office in town and we'll see what we can do."

Once back in Callahan, they met in the real estate office. Everyone was hot, tired and cross from the long ride back to town. Apparently Joe Collins had thought this entire transaction over.

He sat down at his desk and mopped his brow once more.

"Just what is YOUR interest in this sale, sir?" He hated to give up without a fight.

Roarc put his hands on Joe Collins' desk, then leaned over to answer.

"I'm about to marry this lady. When she is my wife, we'll see how this transaction pans out. Perhaps a law suit will solve the problem."

Joe Collins gave up. He certainly didn't relish a law suit. No telling what might come to light in that instance. He nodded.

"I see. Wait a moment please." He went into the back room of his office, then returned with a handful of cash. "You have the deed?"

Roarc handed it to the man. He looked it over, then counted out a stack of bills covering Will's investment in the shoddy piece of land. Roarc counted the bills, then nodded his head in agreement.

"Thanks. But you need to think your advertising over. Grounds for fraud may be in the offing if you don't make some changes." He tipped his hat and escorted Mylena from the office.

He steered her directly to the bank. Roland Hamilton saw them come in.

Boyd seemed to be out again he noted. With a scowl Roland muttered to himself.

"That boy needs some discipline. He's gone more than he's here. He's probably out courting that red-headed librarian again. I need to speak to him about this."

He held out a welcoming hand to Roarc and nodded politely to Mylena. Ah-ha, Rhynhart had come in to pay off his mortgage after all he mused silently.

But Roarc introduced Mylena stating that she wanted to open an account in the bank.

Surprised, Roland escorted them to the nearest teller with a flourish, then he excused himself and returned to his office. But he couldn't help peeking out to see the outcome of that transaction.

Mylena folded the papers verifying her savings account. She stuffed them carefully inside her handbag with a smile.

"Roarc, thank you. I would never have had the nerve to stand up to that Joe Collins like you did. I appreciate it."

"You know, it's unfair but I find there are those who will take advantage of a woman alone. I suspected this might be one of those times." He smiled as he folded her hand in the crook of his elbow as they walked along.

Roarc was taciturn for several days after their return from town. Mylena watched with worried eyes. Even Mose had lost his usual bantering manner. What could be wrong?

Late one evening Rian came wailing to the back door. He seldom cried so Mylena was alarmed. Was he hurt?

"What is it, Rian?" She was quick to respond by meeting him at the door.

"It's my teeth. They're coming out!" He wailed even louder.

"Well, let's see." She sat him down on the back porch to take a look. Sure enough one tooth was leaning back crookedly. It was very loose. She lifted a handkerchief from her pocket and clasped the offending tooth carefully. It came out in the handkerchief along with a drop of blood. She held it up for Rian to see. He was alarmed as tears rolled down his fat little cheeks.

"See—this is called a baby tooth. Coming in right behind it is a big tooth that will last you all your life. Your baby teeth are supposed to come out one by one. Next week the other front tooth may need to be pulled too."

Rian examined the small tooth with curiosity.

"Will all my teeth come out?"

"Yes, but only one at a time. They will be replaced by the new teeth that are waiting inside your gums to come in to stay." She tried to explain this natural phenomenon so he could understand it.

"Will it hurt?"

"Did his one hurt?"

"No—but . . . ."

"Well neither will the others. You will just have to be careful biting apples or chicken legs until your new teeth come in. Don't you remember how the Grady boys teeth look? They are all different lengths. That's because their teeth are changing too. We say they are 'snaggle toothed'."

Rian finally giggled. "I just thought it was because they didn't brush their teeth."

"That had nothing to do with it. However you need to take very good care so your teeth will grow straight and strong for when you are a man. By the time you are a teen-ager, your mouth will look so nice girls will begin to smile at you."

"Aw girls! I don't like them!" He avowed with vehemence.

Mylena laughed with glee. "Well we'll see. I have a sneaky suspicion you just might change your mind one of these days."

Late that night Mylena slipped out to the clothes line to hang some garments she had washed out by hand. They should be dry by morning. With so many men around she hated to hang her intimate clothing out for all to see during the day time. Maidenly modesty, she knew but she couldn't help feeling that way.

Pausing as she heard voices, she stopped. Who was out there? Since the fire everyone had been cautious about unexpected noises—especially at night. She stood still to listen. It was Mose talking to Roarc at the windmill.

"Well, boy, have you decided what you're gonna do about the paying your mortgage?"

"No—I haven't."

"Well now that Mylena has some money, why don't you borrow from her?"

"Oh no!" Roarc was vehement. "That's her legacy from her father and her first husband.

I would never touch that. That idea is out of the question!"

"Well you're gonna marry her. I'll bet she would agree in a minute."

"No Mose! I said I would never do that. I'll just have to think of something else."

"If that rat hadn't burned the wheat crop we'd be fine. It was a good crop this year—the best ever to my way of thinkin'." Mose groused these words sourly.

"I know. But that's just the way it is now."

The two of them parted as Mylena stayed still as a statue beside the lilac bush in the back yard. She couldn't believe what she had just heard. She waited until Mose disappeared in the bunk house and Roarc headed back to the barn. No wonder he was acting to worried. What could she do? Her thoughts were in a whirl as she slipped back into the house and made her way to bed. But it was a long time before she slept.

CHAPTER 14

Mylena sat down beside the churn. She was almost out of butter so it was time to churn again. As she lifted the paddle up and down, her thoughts went up and down as well. How could she make Roarc take some of the money he had helped her retrieve? Why was he so stubborn?

Grady came riding into the yard. He came to the back door and called for Roarc.

Mylena answered.

"He's down at the corral working with Princess and her colt I think. Maybe you'll find him down there."

"Good." He disappeared in that direction while Mylena continued her thinking.

Sure enough the men were working with the blooded horses. Roarc had hoped to begin a string of blue-blooded stock to sell. So far he had only produced Rocket but he had hopes of more in the future. However, if he couldn't even pay his mortgage this year, how could he ever hope to buy any more blooded animals? He was tired and dispirited.

Grady hailed him from the gate.

"Yo, Grady, what's up?" Roarc stopped his training and tossed the reins to Mose.

"I just came from town. I've got some news. Let's go into the tack room."

In the privacy of the little work room he opened up.

"I was just at the livery stable in town and there's a couple of men in Callahan looking for some blood horses. I don't know if you're ready to sell Rocket or not—but they might be interested.

They look like bonafide buyers."

"Why don't we go talk to them?" Roarc was turning away to saddle Arrow as he talked.

Soon the two of them were riding out as dust billowed behind them.

Mylena lifted three loaves of fresh bread from the oven. With the fresh butter she had churned that morning, supper would be a feast. The noise of hooves reverberating along the road caught her attention. She moved to the window to peer out.

Roarc and Grady were riding with two strangers as they headed for the corral. Who could that be? She turned to check on Rian who was busy working on his ciphers at the kitchen table.

After a while Roarc came to the back door.

"Mylena?" he called softly. "Do you have enough supper for two guests"

She went swiftly to answer.

"Yes, I think so. Are we having two guests?"

"Yes ma'am—and thank you." He loped back toward the barn.

Quickly she surveyed her food. If she sliced some ham, then added the potatoes and onions Roarc was so fond of, she would have plenty. For a sweet they could have fresh bread, butter and some of the peach preserves she had bought at Dickens store last month.

Talk and laughter around the supper table was a pleasure for Mylena. Roarc had been so quiet lately it was a joy to hear his deep laughter boom out once more.

She had no idea what was going on but—she liked it! She had taken Rian outside for a quick picnic beneath the big old cottonwood tree. He always liked that. He was such a chatter-box she didn't want him interfering with whatever Roarc was planning. She understood his dilemma now.

At the end of the meal the men adjourned to the front porch to smoke and talk. Mose joined them but Mylena could not make out what they were saying. She had Rian busy closing up the chickens for the night. As she put away the last plate in Lavina's hutch, the two visitors came in to thank her for an excellent meal. Roarc had introduced them but she had been too flustered to remember names.

Then they were bidding them all goodnight and China was riding to accompany them back to town. They were unfamiliar with the road so

Roarc felt they deserved an escort. He came back inside rubbing his hands together and smiling.

"If all goes well we may have our problem solved."

"What do you mean?" Mylena was curious. Who were those men?

"Just for luck, let me tell you about it tomorrow. Nothing is for sure yet."

He took her into his arms for a long moment, then he kissed her goodnight and left for the barn once more.

Back in Callahan, China pointed out the hotel and bid the two visitors goodnight as well. Then he took himself off to sleep in the livery stable with his horse.

The two gentlemen entered the hotel where Nora Davis was presiding at the desk.

"Good evening. We would like two rooms please."

"Oh? Where are you from?" Nora was curious as usual.

"The city," the older man answered as he signed his name to the guest register.

"How long will you be staying?" Still full of questions, she persisted.

"Two days at the most," he replied shortly as he turned away. Nosy witch!

Nora handed the younger man two keys, then watched them as they climbed the stairs to find their rooms. Hmm. She'd give a pretty to know what they were doing in town. She turned the guest register around to read their names—Paul Easton and Dave Easton—hmmm.

Morning found Roarc up earlier than usual. He was out and about aided by Mose.

Before Mylena had finished clearing the table after breakfast with Rian, she heard riders approaching once more. She peeked out the window to find China and the two strangers riding in.

She put her hands on her hips in thought. She'd better fry a couple of chickens and make a double recipe of biscuits for she would bet a wooden nickel they would be here for dinner today.

Putting actions to her thoughts, she had Rian catch two fat fryers as she started her day.

"Mr. Rhynhart, being a visitor in your home, and on your ranch, has been a pleasure. It has been good to do business with you. We'll see you tomorrow at the depot in town."

Compliments to Mylena on her noon meal were extravagant but left her smiling. Roarc shook their hands a final time as he saw them off. They would have no trouble finding their way back to town now that they had made the trip several times. He watched as they disappeared in the distance.

Then he came inside to stand beside Mylena for a moment. Suddenly he put his bronzed hands at her waist and swung her around three times.

"Honey, we made it! Now we can get married!" He kissed her long and hard.

Laughing as he released her, she asked what in the world he was talking about.

"I sold them Rocket. He brought far more than I thought he would. Now our money worries are over!"

"Married? When, Roarc?"

"How about next Friday?. Will that give you time to get ready? Your dress should be finished by now. What do you say?"

Mylena was overwhelmed for a few moments. Friday? Could she?

"But Roarc, I don't want a fancy wedding. I just want to go to the church and be married by the minister there. I don't want a big party."

"Neither do I, sweetheart. If you agree, I'll set it all up tomorrow when I go into town."

Mylena nodded her head in agreement, her eyes shining in delight.

"Now I need to go make the final arrangements for transporting Rocket to the railroad loading chute. We'll talk more about this tonight." With a final kiss, he was out the door.

Rian seemed to be Mose's shadow as the final goodbyes were said to Rocket. Rian was not pleased but he understood that the colt had to go. Mose explained it all in detail. That was what he had been raised for. He would be well-treated and trained by professionals in his new surroundings.

Rian shook his tawny head in acknowledgment—but he didn't like it.

Mylena went to delve into her trunk once more. She still had a few garments she had never worn here in Colorado. They would make up a very satisfactory trousseau. She held them up and whirled before her mirror in delight. She would really be Roarc's wife. She couldn't believe it.

She stopped for a moment. She felt sure he would be a very different lover than Will had ever been.

She blushed in delight as she wondered just how it would be to be held in his hard arms all night.

Clint, Sim and Roarc left early the next morning for the railroad with Rocket between them. He was fine as long as another horse was beside him. Upon their arrival at the railroad loading chute, Sim guided his horse up the ramp into the waiting boxcar. With a shake of his head, Rocket followed obediently with no trouble. You never knew with these blooded horses what they might decide to do. However Rocket had always been easily manageable. This had been one of his best selling points. Sim would ride with him all the way to Colorado Springs where they would change trains for Denver, his final destination. Then Sim would make his way home from Denver. He was looking forward to the trip. He would enjoy seeing the Easton's spread there.

Once the young horse was loaded, the train huffed and puffed its way to the station in town where it would pick up its passengers. Roarc and Clint rode into town where they bade a final goodbye to the Eastons and assured them the horse was safely aboard. They too boarded the train with friendly waves as Roarc stood watching the train until it was out of sight. Then he walked toward the bank.

He ignored Boyd seated at his desk out front and continued on to visit with Roland in his inner sanctum. He had heard around town that the Hamiltons were anticipating his inability to pay his mortgage this year. He wondered what they had planned to do. Ignoring this question, he produced the money to clear his account. Surprised, Roland rose to shuffle the bills about on his desk, then he called a teller to come and take it away to count.

"It's all there, I assure you."

Roarc didn't stay to chat. He had other things to do. After depositing the remainder of his funds, he returned to the depot to purchase tickets to Colorado Springs on Friday with a return on Monday. He would surprise Mylena with a wedding trip. Next he visited the town's only jewelry store to buy a solid gold wedding ring. Finally he rounded up the minister to reserve the church for Friday at eleven o'clock. That would give them time to have the wedding and get to the railroad station at just the right time.

The next day he took Mylena to town to get her wedding clothes. A final modeling of her white suit was taken care of quickly. It was a beautiful outfit.

"Now, dearie, did you get a hat?" Jessie was all smiles. It was such a happy day.

"No! I'll do that right now." Mylena rushed next door to order a matching hat. The milliner was Jessie's cousin, tall, skinny and old-maidish. But she was a whiz with feathers, ribbons and lace. She sat Mylena down and surveyed her from all angles, then she began. Soon a confection of felt, ribbons and lace emerged just to fit Mylena's head. Mylena was delighted and carried the hat in a round box to the buggy Roarc had waiting.

"Anything else?" he asked as he turned the buggy for the return trip back to the ranch.

"Oh yes! I must tell Louise! She will want to be there!" Mylena was out of the buggy again and racing to the doctor's office where Louise and the doctor were sharing a pot of tea during a lull in their busy day. She burst in the door.

They rose as one expecting some kind of medical emergency. They were pleasantly surprised to see Mylena.

"Come in, dear. Are you all right?" Louise was, as usual, delighted to see her.

"Yes, Louise, the wedding is Friday morning. You have to be there!" Mylena was out of breath in her excitement but she managed to explain all the details to the waiting pair.

"We'll close the office for the morning." Dr. Sims was most cordial as they both agreed to share the happy day. Louise planned to be the first to tell Nora Davis the news.

With this final visit, Roarc and Mylena ambled home with smiles on both their faces.

Clint and Walt had planned to leave for Texas the next day but they decided to postpone the trip until after the wedding. They didn't want to miss that.

Friday dawned sunny and crisp. Mylena was glad her white suit was of soft wool—just right for the temperature of the day. Her hat sat jauntily atop her pouf of sable curls as she closed the door and joined the group assembled by the front porch waiting for the bride to appear. Then, with Roarc, Mylena and Rian in the buggy, with Mose, Clint, Walt and China on horseback, they rode to Callahan.

There was quite a crowd waiting inside the little church as Roarc and Mylena approached with Rian in tow. At their appearance the old organ wheezed out a semblance of the wedding march as Nora Davis pumped the pedals with vigor. The minister was waiting at the end of the aisle. It looked a mile long to Roarc as he swallowed nervously. He was not used to being on display—but he would do this for Mylena if it killed him.

They walked slowly down the aisle with Rian right behind them. Mose tried to distract the little boy to no avail. Rian stopped to answer.

"Not right now, Mose. We're getting married." He continued up the aisle behind the bridal couple and stood with them during the entire ceremony.

At last they exchanged loving looks as they said their "I dos"; Roarc slipped the golden circle on Mylena's finger to her delight.

"You may now kiss your bride," intoned the little minister.

And Roarc did.

The organ wheezed once more and Roarc, with his arm about Mylena, turned Rian about to accompany them to the back door of the church. But Nora rose to announce there would be wedding cake at the hotel dining room immediately following the ceremony. The entire group moved to the hotel for a party. Surprised, the bridal couple followed along amid congratulations and good wishes all around.

The dining room was decorated with white streamers. In the center of the room a round table covered by a floor-length table cloth stood in regal splendor. A bouquet of flowers was placed beside a large white wedding cake. Nora and Louise had been quite busy it seemed.

Soon Mylena and Roarc found themselves cutting the cake and sampling the first piece. Rian stood nearby awaiting his turn.

"Where you going on the train?" Nora, ever inquisitive, asked.

"I'm taking my bride to Colorado Springs for three days. I think she deserves a wedding trip." Roarc spoke quietly and shot a fond look at Mylena standing across the room.

At last, in the crush of the celebration, Roarc looked at his watch. It was time to head out for the train station. He moved to her side and touched her arm.

"It's time to go, Mylena. Let's say our goodbyes quickly now."

"Go? Go where?"

"It's a surprise wedding trip to Colorado Springs on the train. Let's go!"

"But what about our luggage?"

"Remember I told you to pack a bag? The boys have already put it on the train so come on! Everything is all planned."

Happily bewildered Mylena followed his lead as Rian trailed right behind them. Once at the station, Roarc began shaking hands with all his men with instructions as to what to do while he was gone for three days.

He bent down to hug Rian goodbye. The little boy immediately burst into loud wails. He sobbed uncontrollably. His feelings were hurt. Besides he had never ridden on a train . . . .

"But, Papa, we just got married. Now I wanta go too!"

"Not now, son, it's our honeymoon . . . . " Roarc began.

But the little boy grabbed his father about his neck and held on for dear life sobbing.

Mylena's heart was touched.

"Wait—why not let him come along as well. He won't be any trouble. After all we are a family now. We can stay together." Mylena's soft voice finally convinced Roarc.

"Well—let me get another ticket right quick. He won't have any clothes . . . . "

"Yes I will, Papa. I saw you packing and I put my clothes right in there under yours. I heard you say we were going on our honeymoon. I didn't know what that was—but I was going too."

The entire crowd burst into laughter.

Mylena and Roarc waved from the train as it pulled out from the station. Rian waved longest of all. Roarc guided them inside the passenger car to find seats. Rian was in front. He looked all about, then made his announcement.

"We're going on our honeymoon."

The entire car full of passengers burst into laughter.

Roarc grabbed the boy's shoulder and set him in a seat quickly. He shook his head as he grinned at Mylena's rosy face.

"This was your idea, lady."

Rian was fascinated by the movement of the train as the scenery whizzed by. The blue mountains came ever closer until they finally arrived in the train depot at Colorado Springs. Mylena had never been here either as they looked about in amazement. People were coming and going in all directions as their luggage was unloaded. Roarc hired a "hack", as they were called in the city, to take them to the hotel. It was in the center of town reached by red brick streets.

The hotel proved to be a grand edifice with marble floors and gold columns beneath crystal chandeliers. Rian was in too much awe to comment. He was too busy looking. Mylena was almost as bad as she held his hand while Roarc checked them in.

"This way to the elevator," Roarc came at last to lead them farther into the building.

Once inside the elevator, Rian was alarmed.

"Is this a cage, Papa?"

"Well—in a way . . . . " Roarc said as they began to move. Rian held Mylena's hand tightly. When the elevator stopped, he grabbed his middle in alarm. But when Roarc stepped out into the long hotel hallway, both Mylena and Rian followed immediately. Rian watched the elevator door close slowly. He didn't quite understand that thing.

Roarc unlocked the door of their room. They entered to find it large, draped with heavy curtains over the windows and carpeted in a red rose designed rug. The room was centered by a huge four poster bed with curtains for privacy. At the foot of the high bed, was the divan the desk clerk had assured Roarc would be ample to accommodate their child. He hoped so.

After inspecting the room, Roarc made a suggestion.

"Why don't we go for a walk around the block while we wait for our luggage. It will be delivered while we're gone." This proved to be agreeable with everyone so they again entered the mysterious elevator. The ride down was even more exciting for Rian as he complained of falling.

Outside the city gas lights were beginning to come on lit by men with long tapered lighters. Rian had to stop and watch this for a while. Roarc held Mylena's hand as they walked along the crowded street. Around a corner was a barber shop with a spinning red, white and blue sign. Again Rian was fascinated. Farther along they spotted a mercantile although this one was much more elegant than the one in Callahan. Rian wanted to go in and shop.

"Not today. We'll be here tomorrow. We can look around then." Roarc was firm in his admonition. He was a bit piqued. This was not exactly the honeymoon he had envisioned.

Once around the block with all its sights Roarc made another decision.

"It's time to head back to the hotel. Let's have supper in the dining room there."

This met with approval all around as they trouped back in the direction they had come.

There a surprise awaited them.

CHAPTER 15

Standing in the lobby was Mose. He was dressed in his best suit, as he had been at the wedding, and he was carrying a valise. He turned as they approached.

"Mose! You came!" Rian ran to the man and threw his arms about his waist. Mose looked a bit shame-faced but he grinned his gamin grin. He clasped Rian in a hug as if they had been parted for weeks instead of hours.

"Mose? What are you doing here?" Roarc asked. He and Mylena were flabbergasted.

"Well—it's your honeymoon and all. I thought I'd come along too and take care of Rian here in the city. He and I will have a room all our own."

"We will?" Rian was delighted to see the older man. They were close buddies.

Roarc grinned. He could see right through Mose's motives. He wanted them to have some time alone together. Bless his heart!

"I decided I wanted to see the zoo the newspaper says is here in Colorado Springs. How about you, Rian? Want to go with me?"

Rian jumped up and down in glee.

"Sure I do! Will we see lions and tigers?"

"Maybe—I won't know until we get there."

"Will there be an elephant too?"

"We'll go first thing in the morning and find out." Mose pocketed his room key and sent his valise upstairs with a porter.

"We're about to have supper in the dining room. Come join us." Roarc was so pleased to see Mose he could have hugged him himself.

Everything was so exciting Mylena could never remember what she ate that night. She kept thinking of the evening ahead when she would be alone with Roarc at last. Her breath caught in her throat as she thought of finally sharing his bed.

At last the meal was finished and they rose to make their way to their rooms. Rian regaled Mose with tales of "the cage" that would take them upstairs. Mose responded as if he had never seen an elevator before and the two were off for a rollicking evening.

"Let's see what Rian brought to wear," Roarc said as he unlocked their door. Rian ran to paw through the jumble of clothing inside the bag that had been delivered to the room. He emerged with a clean shirt, a pair of socks and clean under pants.

"Well it looks like we may be doing a bit of shopping tomorrow after all." He was amused in spite of himself. His boy was something.

Mose spoke up.

"I thought Rian and I would ride the train back to Callahan late tomorrow evening so he may not need any more clean clothes."

Roarc nodded in agreement as Rian clapped his hands. He was ready to ride the train again.

Once they had seen Mose and Rian off, Roarc locked the bedroom door and tossed the key atop a marble table nearby. He went to Mylena and lifted off her hat. He looked deeply into her blue eyes and whispered.

"Hello Mrs. Rhynhart. I think we're alone at last." He placed a tender kiss on her rosy mouth. He followed with caresses to her temple, her cheek and beneath her ear.

"Our lives have been like tangled vines growing in abandon through the years. Now we can train them to blend as we share our love in making a home together."

Mylena smiled.

"I didn't know you were such a philosopher . . . . "

"I'm not," he growled softly. "Would you like first turn at the sink while I take off my boots?"

"Yes, please," Mylena responded with a smile as she turned to select a few things from her own luggage. She stepped behind the ornate screen and began to remove her clothing. A tall ewer filled with hot water plus a matching basin were luxuries she wasn't used to. Donning a white batiste gown, and leaving her sable curls swirling across her shoulders, she stepped out.

But Roarc, barefoot now, caught her once more in a fierce embrace. He nuzzled her neck and whispered once again.

"I won't be long. Don't fall asleep!"

Mylena giggled. As if she WOULD fall asleep in her wedding night!

Roarc released her and disappeared behind the ornate screen himself.

Mylena slipped between the crisp sheets and lay thinking. She felt as if this really was her first wedding night. This time she was madly in love with the man who would claim her for his own before morning light awakened them.

Soon Roarc slipped in bed beside her. He took her in his arms and growled softly.

"My Mylena, I thought this time would never come . . . . "

In a soft whisper she answered, "I know" just before his mouth claimed hers.

THE END

BIOGRAPHY

LaVerne Shaw is a westerner through and though. she loves writing tales about the old west – bygone days that live only in memory now. Add a mix of romance – just a hint of mystery – and she is off and running with a new story.

A native New Mexican, five generations of her family have roots in this western soil. She and her husband have traveled extensively but still find New Mexico home.

You will often find her browsing in the nearest book store or checking out the local library – but never far from her computer.